SANTA SOLDIER BEAR

SPECIAL OPS SHIFTERS: L.A. FORCE

MEG RIPLEY

SHIFTER NATION

Copyright © 2020 by Meg Ripley
www.redlilypublishing.com

All rights reserved. Printed in the United States of America. No part of this book may be used or reproduced in any manner whatsoever without written permission except in the case of brief quotations embodied in critical articles or reviews.

This book is a work of fiction. Names, characters, businesses, organizations, places, events and incidents either are the product of the author's imagination or are used fictitiously. Any resemblance to actual persons, living or dead, events, or locales is entirely coincidental.

Disclaimer

This book is intended for readers age 18 and over. It contains mature situations and language that may be objectionable to some readers.

CONTENTS

SANTA SOLDIER BEAR

Chapter 1	3
Chapter 2	18
Chapter 3	34
Chapter 4	47
Chapter 5	60
Chapter 6	72
Chapter 7	92
Chapter 8	105
Chapter 9	117
Chapter 10	128
Chapter 11	147
Chapter 12	158
Chapter 13	179
Austin	189
Also by Meg Ripley	197

SANTA SOLDIER BEAR

SPECIAL OPS SHIFTERS: L.A. FORCE

1

"I'M A LITTLE NERVOUS ABOUT SHOWING UP LIKE THIS." Roman glanced away from the busy rush-hour traffic and down at the Santa suit he'd put on at Amar's behest. He'd always said he'd do anything for a fellow soldier, but this was a little much. The crimson velvet outfit was rimmed in brilliant white fur that was far too warm for southern California.

"Don't worry about it," Amar said in his headset, the voice familiar from his days in the service. "We decided to have this party to really kick off the Christmas season, and I promised the rest of the Force that there would be a surprise. It'll be a blast."

"Dude, easy for you to say. You're not dressed in a getup like this," Roman growled. He followed the GPS's directions, turning onto a road lined with palm trees and impressive homes. It was a far cry from what he'd gotten used to between his time in the Army and the time he'd spent in Wyoming. "When you said you wanted me to come down to spend Christmas with you, I didn't realize you'd be suckering me into playing Santa."

"Come on, don't be such a stick in the mud. I didn't want you to be alone for the holidays after everything that went down this year."

Roman paused, knowing what he was about to say, but he let it go.

"You'll have fun," Amar promised. "Are you almost here?"

"Yeah, I think so. This is one hell of a place." He pulled his rented truck to a stop in front of an enormous modern home. Covered porches stuck out at all angles, taking advantage of the stunning view. From the maps Roman had looked at earlier, he knew it butted up close to some of the nature preserves in the area, making it a great spot for shifters. The house was far different from the ranches and farmhouses he was used to seeing back in Wyoming, where he'd moved six months ago. It didn't look much like Christmas, either, despite the giant plastic candy canes sticking out of the flowerbed along the walkway, but he was happy to spend time with Amar. It would be good to see him and to meet this Special Ops Shifter Force that he'd talked so much about.

"I see you out there. Just wait a few minutes, then come straight through the front door. I'll make sure it's unlocked."

"If you say so. I hope this goes well, but you owe me either way." The last thing Roman wanted was to be the center of attention, but there was no way to avoid it. Everyone would be looking at him, whether he was just Amar's friend or Santa.

"Big time. Now get your ass in here." There was a click as Amar hung up.

With a sigh, Roman hopped out of his truck. The rental agency had looked at him strangely when he'd turned down the sedans and coupes they'd offered. Even though he didn't have hay or fencing materials to haul around right now, Roman was used to something a little more functional. He opened the back door and pulled out the velvet bag full of packages, praying no one drove by. Even though he didn't know anyone in L.A., he'd still rather be seen by as few people as possible in this getup. Tugging on the hat that matched the outfit, he headed for the front door and ambled in as Amar had asked.

Roman got past the festive wreath on the front

door, covered in jingle bells that greeted him merrily, and headed straight into the massive open floorplan. Someone had gone all out with the decorations. Garland twined down the banister, and white lights twinkled from every horizontal surface. A colossal Christmas tree dripping with ornaments reached up to the highest point on the ceiling, and a pile of perfectly wrapped presents had already been placed under it. The stockings along the mantel looked as though they'd been hung with plenty of care, showing their owners' names printed in silver glitter. The scent of cinnamon and pine permeated the air, and old holiday music filtered through the room.

Heads turned to stare, and Roman remembered who he was supposed to be. He might as well make the most of this. "Ho ho ho! I hear there are some good boys and girls here tonight!"

"Santa?" A little face peeked out from behind the leg of a dark-haired woman, his blue eyes full of wonder, hope, and a little fear.

The boy's mother looked around the room. Getting a wink from Amar, she took her son's hand and brought him over. "Yes, sweetie. It's Santa."

Roman bent down to look at the boy. He tipped his head from one side to the other, pretending to think. "You're Lucas, aren't you?"

"My name!" Lucas squealed. "That's me!"

As ridiculous as he'd felt in the red, fur-lined outfit and big boots, seeing the delight on Lucas's face made it all worth it. His chest heated with a warmth that had nothing to do with the costume. "I hear you've been a very good boy this year. You know, Lucas, I'm pretty sure I have a present for you in this bag."

The boy didn't waste time, darting over to an empty wingback chair near the fireplace and patting the seat. "Sit, Santa! Sit!"

"*Please* have a seat," his mother corrected gently.

Roman did as the boy asked, sitting and digging through the bag until he found a gift labeled for Lucas. "My elves and I have been keeping a close eye on you, so I know you deserve this, buddy. Here you go!"

Lucas grabbed the box and immediately fell to the floor as he ripped off the paper. His face illuminated with glee as he tore a strip from the end of the package. His tiny fingers went searching for further purchase to continue the unveiling of his gift.

Everyone was staring, but Roman felt a specific set of eyes on him more than the rest. He dragged his gaze through the room, trying to be casual as he looked. His chest tightened as he spotted a gorgeous woman near a buffet table. Her curly red hair had been tamed into a high bun, a sprig of holly stuck festively in the side, but Roman could tell it was wild and unruly when she let it down. Her tortoiseshell glasses made her look prim, but the pale brown eyes behind them were intriguing. As beautiful as her face was, Roman couldn't help letting his eyes drift down to take in the gentle curves of her slim body. His polar bear fluxed and swelled inside him, and if he'd let it rule, he would've been at her side in a flash.

"I believe Santa brought gifts for everyone else, too," Amar said, dragging Roman's attention back to the real reason he was there. He gestured toward the overflowing bag of gifts.

"Of course!" Roman tore his gaze away from the redhead and began pulling more presents out of the bag, glad to focus on something besides that temptress across the room. He lifted a small box wrapped in green paper and tied with a gold bow. "Emersyn?"

The boy's mother took the gift, giving Amar a smile. "That's very kind of you, Santa."

"Merry Christmas." Roman's cheeks burned under the ridiculous white beard. He'd spent his entire adult life in the service, and while he'd pulled plenty of crazy stunts, none of them had made him feel like the spotlight was on him as much as this. Had Amar told anyone else that he'd set this whole thing up? Were they all wondering who this mysterious stranger was? It'd be easier if he could've just come in, said hi, had some eggnog, and blended into a corner somewhere. He was just there to visit, after all, not to play the jolly old elf from the North Pole.

Purposely, Roman retrieved a specific package from the bag. "This one is for Amar."

He came through the crowd, one hand in his pocket and a big smile on his face. "It's good to see you, Santa."

Roman shook the package in his hand, holding onto it tightly. "I'm not sure you actually made the good list this year, little boy," he warned.

"Sit!" Lucas was only halfway through tearing the colorful paper off his toy train, but he stood and eagerly patted Roman on the knee. "Sit, Uncle Amar!"

Emersyn pressed a hand to her lips, not quite covering her smile. "I think he wants you to sit on Santa's lap and tell him you've been good. He's already been to the mall once, and it's made quite the impression on him."

Lucas nodded eagerly and patted Roman's knee once again.

Roman knew how serious Amar was. He was never the type to head out on a weekend of leave and party until it was time to report for PT on Monday morning. He was the only one who ever came back sober, as far as Roman could remember. He was a stodgy old dragon, and if he was going to make Roman act like a fool in front of these strangers, then he'd have to do the same. He patted his knee, right next to where Lucas's warm little hand still rested. "Come on, Amar. Perhaps you've done some good that my elves aren't aware of. Why don't you tell me about it? Santa is always ready to listen."

To the rousing cheers of the rest of the party, Amar sat. "I'm going to get you for this."

"You already did," Roman reminded him.

Amar leaned in close, concern wrinkling his brow. "Have you talked to Elizabeth at all?"

Roman let out a low growl, just quiet enough that no one besides Amar could hear it. He was already embarrassed enough. His relationship with Elizabeth hadn't been all that long ago, but it wasn't something he wanted to talk about. If he had it his way, he'd never speak about that time in his life again.

Amar raised a brow. "Point taken."

A blonde woman came through the crowd with her camera held out for pictures. "Smile, Amar! This one's getting framed and put on the wall."

Amar smiled broadly and put his arm around Roman's shoulders for the first shot. In another, Roman shook his gloved finger while Amar pouted. Though he'd felt strange about doing this little Santa gig, Roman quickly forgot how ridiculous he felt and started enjoying himself. It was a little easier to have all eyes on him when he was disguised with a hat and beard.

"Okay, okay," Amar finally said, getting up and gesturing toward the big bag. "I think it's someone else's turn. Katalin, my love, Santa told me he has something for you."

"Is that so?" A striking woman appeared at his side, smiling up at her mate. Her dark hair and eyes were a steep contrast to her porcelain skin and ruby lips. Amar had explained to Roman that his mate was a vampire, but seeing her in the flesh was entirely different than hearing about her. Katalin didn't look like a blood-sucking creature of the night in the slightest.

Roman fished through the bag, finding a slender box wrapped in gold paper. He handed it over, and though the gift said it was from Santa, Katalin only had eyes for Amar as she removed the glittering diamond tennis bracelet.

"I guess this means I've been good this year, too," she commented with a little smile as Amar fastened the bauble around her wrist.

Amar pressed a kiss to the back of her hand. "Very."

Roman turned away from the scene that somehow reminded him of Gomez and Morticia. He pulled out a gift for someone named Gabe, who'd been helping Lucas open his toy train. The man took his present, but he only posed next to Santa for a quick photo before he returned to his son. When Raul and Penny stepped up, Roman could sense how close their mated bond was. He shoved down the bubble of raw envy in his gut and smiled while they stood on either side of him for their photo. Next came Jude. Roman never thought he'd meet someone even more solemn than Amar, but Jude chose not to do a photo at all—even when his mate, Annie, tried to pressure him into it. Reid practically launched himself into Roman's lap and pulled Mali along with him, the two of them squealing and laughing like kids as they made faces for the camera. Next came Kent and Alessia, who held hands even while accepting their presents.

As Roman passed out the gifts and became an entertainment source for the adults more than the child in the room, he felt far more in the Christmas spirit than he'd expected to be. He'd doubted his decision to come to L.A. for the holidays more than once, but at that moment, it felt right. He had no doubt that the group Amar had adopted himself into was a good one. They were all sorts of shifters, yet it was clear they had a close sense of family. Roman felt a small pang of jealousy as he pulled the last gift from the bag and read the tag. "This one is for Melody."

His world stopped as that gorgeous redhead glided across the room. Her cheeks turned pink as she accepted the package. "Thank you," she said as her eyes lifted to meet Roman's.

The Christmas tree could've caught on fire at that moment and Roman wouldn't have noticed. He felt his inner polar bear stirring, restless, and hungry. It surged toward her, sending adrenaline blasting through his veins. She'd been intriguing from across the room, but as she stood mere inches away, she was the most magnificent creature he'd ever encountered. Roman could sense her very soul, smooth and cool, yet warm and cozy, like a fire on a midwinter evening. He opened his mouth, feeling as though he was supposed to say something, but apparently, he'd forgotten the English language.

"Sit on his lap and we'll get a picture!" someone called.

"Oh, um..." Melody hesitated, looking from Roman to her friend and back again. "We really don't have to do that."

"Come on!" another voice urged.

"I'm sure Santa wouldn't mind," Amar said with another wink.

Damn him. If he had any idea what had been going on in Roman's mind, he wouldn't have said that. Actually, he would've. The dragon could be mischievous like that, and Roman wouldn't put it past him to push his friend into something he thought was good for him. He didn't want to make Melody any more uncomfortable than she was, though. "It's entirely up to you."

"Sit, Mel'dy!" Lucas was at Roman's side once again, quite the little coordinator for being the youngest in the room.

Melody glanced at the boy, and her shoulders visibly sagged as her heart melted and she gave in. "All right, but just for a second."

Roman put out his arm as she bent down and perched on his knee, a smile pasted onto her face. "I'm so sorry," she whispered through her teeth.

"It's quite all right." God, she had no idea just how all right it was! Roman had to wonder why he'd never thought about dressing up as Santa for a Christmas party before if this was the way to get hot chicks to sit on his lap. He could feel the strength of her muscles and the softness of her curves as she braced herself against him, looking this way and that for everyone who wanted to snap a photo. Roman didn't know her at all, but it was clear that the crowd was having just as much fun with Melody as they had with Amar.

"Smile! No, like you mean it!" Penny called out.

"Aww, you blinked!" This came from Annie, who frowned at her phone. "Quick! Let's try again."

"Scoot in closer! Let's get one of those funny, cuddly shots," Alessia said, gesturing with her hand. "Kind of a 'Santa, Baby' vibe."

"I'm sorry," Melody whispered as she scooched further onto his lap. Her bottom inched up closer, moving from his knee to his hip.

"Not a problem," Roman said through his teeth. But it was. All the air had squeezed out of his lungs, leaving him in a vacuum. His polar bear was going wild inside him, inciting his human body into a riotous state. He was hardly in control at all, and there was a little less room in his costume now that his body started responding to the sexy woman sitting on his lap. If the situation had been different, if they hadn't had an entire room full of people staring at them, he would've stripped her bare and devoured her right then. The thought only made his pulse race faster, and he felt like a teenager trying to figure out how to get up from his desk in the middle of class without everyone noticing what he was carrying around in his pants.

Several more photos were snapped. His muscles were stiff and achy as he fought to control his body, but he thought he was in the clear as some of the eagerness died down. This was the last gift to be handed out, and soon, the party would be directed toward some other activity. Roman didn't know what that would be, and he didn't care—as long as he could get out of there with some of his dignity intact.

Then Emersyn shook her head. "I'm not getting the right angle. Can you turn to the side a bit?"

Melody did as she was asked, pressing her behind right up against his rock-solid erection. She stiffened, her back straightening quickly.

Damn it. There was no getting away from it now

and no taking it back. She knew, and she didn't seem too happy about it. Roman waited just long enough for someone to take the picture, knowing that too quick of a reaction would only make things worse.

"You know what, I think Santa's done for the night." Roman scooped Melody up off his lap. Even for that brief second, she felt perfect in his arms. He had to let that thought go as he grabbed the empty velvet gift bag and held it strategically in front of his tent. He waved erratically as he headed for the front door. "Merry Christmas to all, and to all a good night!"

He barreled toward the door, feeling heat rising in waves off his skin. Melody had noticed, but had anyone else? Would she tell them? He didn't want to know. Escaping out the front, Roman raced over to his truck, wondering why he'd ever agreed to come to L.A. for a visit in the first place—and how he was ever going to go back inside that party and face Melody again.

2

Melody stood in front of the long mirror in her room, pulling the sprig of holly from her hair and unwinding her bun. The tiny piece of greenery had been something she'd intended to stick in a wreath as she worked on the Christmas decorations at Force headquarters, but it worked so well as a hairpiece, she couldn't resist.

She'd already changed into flannel pajama bottoms with reindeer prancing all over them and a snug cotton t-shirt, and she sighed happily as she set the holly on the dresser. "I just love Christmas. I love that warm, fuzzy feeling it gives me inside."

"Even when you're frantically trying to pick out gifts for everyone?" Emersyn asked from the bed, peering over the screen of her laptop. Her hair had been carefully curled for the party, but she'd swept it back into a braid for the evening.

"It's not that bad." Melody grabbed her tablet and flopped onto the bed next to her, kicking her feet up into the air. "After all, there's still plenty of time for online shopping if you really don't want to get out."

"It's not that I don't want to," Emersyn corrected. "In fact, nothing sounds better than just taking a long day visit every mall and store in the city and fill the car up with gifts. I wouldn't mind taking in all the sights and decorations, too, but I just don't have the time. My work at the clinic gets absolutely crazy around the holidays. I don't even know if I'll have much time for Force missions over these next two months."

"That bad, huh?" Emersyn was actually Dr. Emersyn Cruz, and in addition to the work she did with the Force, she ran a clinic in one of the lower-income neighborhoods. She was very passionate about her work, and Melody knew she often stayed there late at night as she helped those who were the worst off. It was because of her work that Melody had begun watching Emersyn's son Lucas, back before either of them had ever even heard of the Special Ops Shifter Force.

"Yeah, but it's like this every year. And every year, we get a bad outbreak of the flu or something else along those lines. I just don't like seeing anyone in pain, you know?"

"I know." Emersyn had one of the biggest, most giving hearts of anyone Melody knew, and it was just one of the many reasons Melody liked her so much. "Oh, check this out. Lucas is really into trains right now. Do you think he'd like this?" Melody turned her tablet around to show the adorable set of train pajamas she'd just found.

Emersyn shook her head, but she was smiling. "Sometimes, I think you know him better than I do, Mel. I don't know what I'd do without you."

"Oh, I don't do anything special," Melody countered. "Lucas and I just hang out while I do my work."

"The very important work of not just caring for Lucas, but keeping the whole Force running smoothly," Emersyn replied with an arched brow.

"I just balance the books." Melody's cheeks were burning. She couldn't believe her luck when Emersyn had secured her a spot at Force HQ, working as both the in-house daycare provider and their bookkeeper. She didn't hate getting to live in a sprawling, spectacular home for free, and she loved the excitement of being so close to the Special Ops vets who fought to keep the many shifter clans in the area safe.

"Bullshit. Even Amar gushes over how organized you are, and you know he's not the kind to let the light bill slip by unnoticed. It's because of you that we have all the groceries and supplies we need. You're the one who did all that insane Martha Stewart Christmas decorating. You were even the one who had the roof repaired last month after the storm. It's like you're the mother to this whole house, and you're amazing at it. Don't let yourself believe anything less."

Melody smiled at her friend. "I'm a firm believer in getting things done, that's all."

"Speaking of getting things done, are you going to do anything about *Roman*?" Emersyn challenged.

Her cheeks heated all over again at the mention of the handsome stranger. "Check out this sale on pocket knives. It's for a limited time, so I'd better stock up while I can. I think the guys will like them."

With one quick movement, Emersyn reached over and snatched the tablet out of Melody's hand. "I'm sure they will, but let's talk about Roman first. There was a connection between the two of you. I could tell."

"Well, I mean, he's a good-looking guy. I could see that, even with the Santa costume on." As a matter of fact, Melody hadn't been able to get that gorgeous face out of her mind all night. She'd gotten a glimpse of Roman after he'd come back in the house, when he'd ditched the big red suit and had brought in his suitcase to get settled in. His hair was dark, and he kept it in a short enough style to keep the curls from being too unruly. It matched the short beard that clung to his face and had been hidden completely by the Santa beard not long before that. Then there were those eyes…

"Yes, that part is obvious. But is there more than that?"

"I mean, I could tell he was, um, definitely attracted to me," Melody admitted. She'd been so shocked when she'd scooted over and discovered that her body hadn't been the only one reacting to their close proximity. "The hard evidence was right there, if you know what I mean."

The two women descended into a fit of giggles.

Melody put her hands to her face, feeling embarrassed for Roman. "It was all my fault! I was practically wiggling around on his lap, trying to accommodate all the pictures everyone wanted to take, and I practically sat right on it!"

"No wonder he got up and left," Emersyn replied, still laughing. "If the other guys know, they're probably giving him hell for it right now."

"Don't get me wrong. It's incredibly flattering. I just wasn't really thinking about it, because I was already feeling put on the spot just by having to sit on some random hot guy's lap." Melody swept her auburn curls out of her face and then wanted to pull them back down again just so she'd have something to hide behind.

"Even grown men can't help those things sometimes," Emersyn said. "Still, I swear I sensed something more than just a physical attraction between the two of you. As soon as you were close to each other, there was this little bubble that surrounded you, and you were the only ones in the room. Is there something you should be telling me?" Emersyn grinned as she tapped her fingers on the edge of the tablet.

Melody hesitated. Emersyn was her best friend. There was no one else in the world she would've rather talked to about this. After all, the connection Melody had felt to Roman had been intense. He was a complete stranger. She didn't know him at all, yet she'd distinctly felt her inner snow leopard wake up and try to leap straight out of her chest. She'd wanted to curl up on his lap and purr, imagining his strong hands stroking through her fur. Melody had never had that sort of reaction to anyone before. She knew what it could mean, but what if she were wrong?

Even if Roman was her mate, she couldn't just upend her life in L.A. She had obligations to the Force, which were important enough, but she was also committed to watching Lucas. Emersyn had just told her how vital she was to everyone there, and Roman lived all the way up in Wyoming, according to Amar. There were too many things to think about, and she was too tired to mull it all over.

"No, nothing's going on there. I was just in a good mood because I had a little too much to drink. We had a great Thanksgiving, and I'm glad everyone agreed to let me do this Christmas kickoff party. I mean, who knows what Christmas itself will end up looking like."

"That's true enough," Emersyn agreed. "I've thought about that a lot, actually. I'd like Lucas to have as traditional of a holiday as possible, but what if a mission comes up? What about all my work at the clinic? Things don't stop just because a date on the calendar says to."

Their conversation turned away from Roman

and back to shopping and planning. Melody showed Emersyn the Christmas wrap she'd recently picked out, and they joked about getting all the members of the Force to dress in matching holiday pajamas for a cute photo.

That part of the conversation made her mind immediately drift back to Roman, wondering what might have gone differently if they'd met some other way. What if he'd walked in and was just introduced as Amar's friend? Would they have found a way to talk at the drinks table or near the tree, getting to know each other while feeling that distinctive connection? Or would he have just been another person she met for a brief moment before he had to return to Wyoming, never to be thought of or seen again? Was there some element of destiny in the way they'd met? Melody shook her head. She'd had too much eggnog to begin with. She just needed to wind down and forget about it until she could think rationally.

"Okay. I'm not even going to look at the total of my online cart, so I'm checking out and heading to bed." Emersyn shut her computer and glanced up. "You all right?"

"Hm? Oh, yeah. Just tired. And a little hungry, surprisingly. I snacked a whole lot, but I didn't really eat a meal." Having made very little progress with her own shopping, she turned off her tablet and set it on her nightstand. "I think I'll head downstairs and raid the fridge."

Emersyn stood and stretched, bracing her feet on the floor and arching into the air like the pantheress she was at heart. Melody had often thought one of the reasons they were so compatible was because they were both felines. "I wouldn't be surprised if some of the others are doing the same. Everyone seems to eat at midnight around here."

"It's not exactly a normal work schedule," Melody agreed. "What about you? You hungry?"

"Nah. I'm heading to bed." She tucked her laptop under her arm.

"I'll be doing the same soon." Melody shoved her feet into her favorite slippers. "I'll check on Lucas before I go to bed."

Emersyn had been heading for the bedroom door, but she turned around and leaned on the frame. "You really are amazing, Melody. You treat my son like he's your own, and no matter how much he interferes with your work, you just roll right along like everything is peachy. Seriously, I don't know how this place would function without you." She padded down the hall to the room she shared with Gabe.

Yeah, but I don't want to think about that right now, Melody thought.

As she descended the stairs, Melody was overcome with the homey feeling of Christmas. The white lights she'd strung along the banister, around the Christmas tree, across the mantle, and on several shelves were the only lighting in the main living area of the house, and they cast a warm, cozy glow that was instantly reflected in her chest as she stepped off the last stair. She hesitated on the last step, just standing there and taking it all in. She slowly moved toward the kitchen, trailing her fingers over the garland on the sofa table. A scrap of something on the carpet caught her eye, and she stooped to pick it up: a piece of wrapping paper from Lucas's gift. It was just a piece of trash now, but it'd brought him so much joy just a few hours ago. Her heart ached for just one more hug from the little boy, but it would have to wait until morning.

Melody didn't bother turning on the light in the kitchen. She knew this place like the back of her hand, and the miniature silver Christmas tree she'd put smack in the middle of the counter gave off plenty of light. It was early in the season, but her favorite Christmas song popped into her head as she opened the fridge, and she couldn't help but sing along. "Santa, baby..."

There'd been tons of food for the party, and she slowly scanned each shelf as she tried to decide what she wanted to eat. Her mouth watered just from the thought of it, and once again, her mind circled back to Roman. "Been an angel all year..." It was late and she was alone, so she allowed herself to move to the music that was consuming her head. A fantasy of Roman in a *much* smaller version of that Santa costume floated through her mind as Melody pulled out a plate of deviled eggs and bent down to get Raul's famous ham from the bottom shelf. "So hurry down the chimney tonight!" She shut the fridge door.

"If you insist."

Melody shrieked before slapping her hand over her mouth and doubling over. "Holy shit, you scared me! How long were you standing there letting me make a fool out of myself?"

He smiled, and the twinkle in his dark eyes wasn't from the Christmas lights. "Long enough. I thought I'd come down for a midnight snack."

Though she had somewhat recovered from the scare, Melody wasn't sure she'd ever recover from seeing Roman standing there like that. His plaid pajama bottoms weren't too dissimilar from what she wore, but his tight-fitting undershirt showed off his sculpted muscles. It was too easy to imagine what it would be like to press her hands against that shirt and feel the heat of his skin through it. Her tongue curled in her mouth as she took a step backward. "Well, there's certainly plenty here."

"So you don't mind if I join you?"

Could he tell that she no longer knew how to breathe? He'd probably seen her shaking her ass in the air, singing a song full of innuendo. Her only hope was that he couldn't read minds and had no idea she'd been thinking about him the entire time. "Sure. Of course. I was actually going to see if there were any good holiday movies on TV, if you'd like to join me for that, too." God, what was she saying?

Roman reached past her with one long, brawny arm and picked up the platter of ham. "That sounds great."

Melody wanted to kick herself as she led the way into the living room. What would they watch? Where would they sit? They'd have to sit close together to share the food. Wait, did that mean anything significant if they were sharing their food? No. She was overthinking this. Just because Roman had incited a feeling inside her that she'd never experienced, one that could be... No. It was just a midnight snack. That was it. It didn't have to mean anything.

"Do you have a favorite?" Roman asked as he set the platter on the coffee table.

"Huh?"

"A favorite Christmas movie."

"Oh. I don't know if I could choose." Melody racked her brain for even a title of a Christmas movie. She loved this time of year, and the movies were a big part of it. There was nothing better than settling in on a cool night to relax and watch an old flick, even if she'd already seen it a hundred times. So why couldn't she come up with even one? "It's hard to say. I like so many of them. Christmas is probably my favorite time of year."

"Then I'm surprised you live in L.A."

"What do you mean?" Melody settled in next to him on the couch, the table in front of them loaded with food. She tried not to think about how close his muscular thigh was to hers.

"It doesn't feel very Christmasy around here. I mean, other than inside the house itself. You guys must've really gone all out when you hired a decorator. If I didn't know there were palm trees swaying in a warm breeze outside, I'd think I was at the North Pole." Roman gestured widely to take in the garland, lights, and baubles.

"We didn't hire a decorator," Melody replied with a laugh. "I did this."

Roman had sat back against the cushions, but he sat up and braced his elbows on his knees. "Really? By yourself?"

"Well, sure." Her face flushed as he looked so intensely into her eyes. She let her own gaze take in his high cheekbones, the long line of his nose, the hardness of his jaw. His dark hair was rumpled, probably from being under that ridiculous Santa hat earlier. The reminder of their initial meeting sent a tingle of energy through her nipples, and she was glad they hadn't bothered turning on the lights. "It was a lot of work, but I'd gladly do it all over again."

"It doesn't bother you to put in all that effort, only to have to take it all back down in a month?" Roman grabbed a slice of ham off the platter, rolled it around a deviled egg, and downed it.

"No way. I love the feeling of Christmas, how it makes you think about home and love and even just being lucky to have a roof over your head and people to be with during the holidays. It's so cozy and warm, and I love the contrast of winter darkness with the twinkling lights. I find it incredibly..." She stalled, realizing the word she was about to say was 'romantic.' That wouldn't work in this situation, not when she was so close to a man like Roman.

"Idyllic?" he filled in for her.

"Yes, you could say that." Melody picked up the remote and turned on the TV, skipping all the available streaming services and opting for plain old antenna television. It was part of the nostalgia for her, remembering when she was a kid and had to catch her favorite movies while they were on. "Oh, *It's a Wonderful Life* just started. Does that work for you?"

"To be honest, I've seen it about a hundred times. In one of the places where I was stationed, a lot of our personal belongings got stalled in transit. Someone had a scratched DVD of this, and it was all we watched, even while we were out in the middle of the desert."

Melody held her finger over the button as she turned to him. Her snow leopard was swirling like an arctic wind inside her, blasting her from the inside out as she admired him. It wasn't just his looks, though she certainly appreciated those. It was the rumble of his voice. It was the way he moved with such ease and confidence. It was the strength and patience he exuded and the fact that he didn't seem to be aware of any of that. "Want me to find something else?"

"No, actually. It'd be nice to see it without a bunch of lines across the screen from a bad DVD." He put his hand over hers to push the remote down.

Her throat tightened completely as a shiver ran up her spine, making goosebumps explode over the back of her neck. This man had an effect on her unlike anything she'd ever felt before. She folded one foot under her knee, trying to anchor herself in reality instead of the fantasies that wouldn't leave her head. "I just have to warn you, I always cry when he finds Zuzu's petals in his pocket."

Roman laughed and scooted a little closer to her, his eyes shining. "You can lean on my shoulder if you need to."

"I just might." Melody smiled as she reached for the ham. This was proving to be the best midnight snack she'd ever had.

3

THE MOVIE WAS GOOD, BUT ROMAN WAS HARDLY paying any attention to it. His polar bear had been on a rampage when he arrived at Force HQ, but sitting there with Melody had soothed it. If he listened to his inner animal at all, then that meant... No. He had to stop himself from shaking his head to rattle the thought from his brain; he didn't want to distract Melody from the movie. But he knew it couldn't be. He would just enjoy the time he had left there—with her—and make the most of it before he headed back to Wyoming.

Melody sniffled as she wiped a tear from the corner of her eye. "I'm sorry. I told you I would cry. It's always the kids that get to me. Even though

George Bailey takes up most of the movie, there's something about seeing him hug his kids with such love and joy at the end that I just can't get past, no matter how many times I see it." She reached forward to get the remote off the table.

Roman admired the long lines of her body as she did so. It was as though his eyes were addicted to her already, lingering on the wild red curls of her hair, the smattering of freckles on her cheeks, and even the way her fingers rested against the soft fabric of her pants. "What about you? Have any kids of your own?"

She rolled her shoulder. "No, and at this point, I kind of figured I wouldn't have any. But I *am* the chief caretaker for Lucas when I'm not doing the bookkeeping for the Force. That little nugget is an absolute dream."

He could see the warmth in her smile when she spoke of the boy. It ignited something inside him, but Roman knew better. He pushed it down again, reminding himself that his night with Melody could be nothing more than casual. "So, that's what your role is in the Force?"

"I'm not really a member of the Force, not in the same way the others are," she explained, sitting back against the couch cushions. The white twinkle lights illuminated her face, making her look as angelic as the tree topper. "I usually refer to myself as being Force-adjacent."

"But you live here, I assume," Roman countered. "It's because of you that Gabe and Emersyn can do their jobs, and I'm sure they appreciate having a numbers person around to balance the books. That's not for everyone." He didn't know why he had such an urge to make her feel she was just as vital as the Force members who physically fought for shifters all over L.A. Amar had explained how everything worked in the Force. He'd even hinted at recruiting him, but he wasn't meant for city life.

"It's still not really the same." She bit her lip, but the corners of her mouth turned up.

Damn, she was cute. His bear swelled inside him when he looked at her, loving every second of being so close to her.

"Shit, it's not like I'm out there doing anything heroic," Melody continued. "Besides, I get the better end of the bargain. I get a little work done, and I get to hang out with Lucas. It means that I at least get to feel like a parent sometimes, even when I'm not. What about you? Any kids?"

It was an innocent enough question. There was

nothing wrong with it. Still, Roman felt that trigger pull inside him. His polar bear roared as he recalled the way he'd been wronged. It still hurt so badly, even months later. The tip of his tongue wiggled against the inside of his teeth as he considered whether or not to answer her. He hardly knew Melody, and it wasn't fair to just spew out his life story and expect her to be able to handle it. "No," he finally said quietly. "No kids."

If she'd noticed his hesitation or the tension that had suddenly built inside his muscles, she didn't let him know. Melody adjusted her position on the couch, inching her knee a little closer to his thigh. "There's just something so magical about kids and the way they absorb everything around them," she mused, gazing up at the ceiling. "Even when we don't think they're paying attention, or we think something must be beyond their grasp, they just turn around and *know*. Like Lucas did this afternoon when he wanted everyone to sit on your lap."

It was too warm in the room. Did everything in L.A. have to be so damn hot? He craved the cool air of Wyoming to ease his soul. It wouldn't make him forget about Melody, though. As much as he wanted to turn and run from this situation, to save himself from looking like a fool, he knew their inner beasts would never let them ignore what had happened. Roman ran a hand through his hair. "Yeah, I guess we need to talk about that."

She turned away, but he could see the smile in the profile of her face. "We don't have to. It was just one of those things."

"If you mean the mere attraction of a man to a woman, then yes." Roman moved closer to her, longing to feel the silky smoothness of her skin under his hand. "But I think there was much more to it than that."

Turning just enough so that she could look at him, Melody raised an eyebrow. "Was there?"

"I think you know." God, he hoped she did. But in everything that Roman knew about shifters, these things weren't simply one-sided. He couldn't have that sort of reaction without her because *she* was part of the equation. The way his bear had gone berserk was a direct reflection of how her animal side was reacting. "There was something far more between us; something neither of us can control."

"I see," she said with a quirky little smile, reaching over and brushing cookie crumbs off the leg of his pants. "So if a girl just wants to sit on Santa's lap and tell him what a good girl she was all year, it has to mean something?"

"Absolutely. Especially if she shares her food with him. And especially if he has a far better time just sitting on the couch with her watching Christmas movies than he ever thought he would." He found himself leaning closer and closer to her as his polar bear urged him to close the distance between them.

"And if she might have felt the same thing, what do you think she should do about it? I mean, considering that they live in completely different parts of the country?" Melody had turned now so that she faced him.

Her face was so close to his, close enough that he only had to lift his hand to touch her cheek. Roman longed to tell her that none of that mattered if they were mates, but he knew it did. There was always something that jumped in the way of happiness, no matter what fate might be trying to say to the contrary. Did Melody want him to just brush off these feelings? Roman couldn't do that.

"You and I both know that a shifter can wait an entire lifetime, just hoping for the chance to run across the one person they're meant to be with. I'm not saying I know what to do about it, but I do know it's there." He swallowed, hardly believing those words were escaping his mouth.

She swallowed. It was a simple motion, but the way it moved her throat was tantalizing. Roman wanted to sink his teeth into it, to reach out with his tongue and touch her skin. He wanted to be a part of her, and he wanted her to know what it was like to be a part of him.

"Are you joining the Force?"

Did she know that Amar had talked to him about it? Roman didn't doubt how tightly knit everyone in that household was, so he wouldn't be surprised if Amar had mentioned it to the rest of them. His old buddy had tried hard, but Roman knew that Sheridan, Wyoming was his true home. He could never be happy in a place like L.A. "No."

Melody swallowed once again. Her lips moved, and for a moment, he thought she might kiss him. Instead, she swayed back ever so slightly. The increase in distance was so slight, but it was like a knife in his heart. "Well, at least we've had tonight," she said quietly. "I've had fun with you, Roman."

He felt as though he'd been trying to hold water in his hands and could only stand by helplessly as he watched it leak through his fingers. Melody was special. She was magical. She was like that Christmas wish that people always talked about in the movies, something you hoped would come true, but you never thought would. All he knew was that he wanted to keep a hold of her as long as possible. "Me, too."

"I'd better put all of this away." Melody reached forward, taking a plate in each hand.

After allowing himself a moment to see the curve of her backside as she stood, Roman joined her in cleaning up.

The two of them operated in a symphony of kitchen noises as they rinsed plates, covered leftovers, and returned everything to the fridge. Even though it felt like an anticlimactic end to what had been a promising evening, Roman found that the simple act of kitchen work was pleasant as long as he got to do it with Melody at his side. He liked the way her hair responded to her motions as she rinsed a dish. He certainly didn't mind seeing her bend over to load plates in the dishwasher. There was something authoritarian and domestic about her as she arranged items in the fridge. It was when he could stand back and realize that everyday chores were turning him on that he knew for sure he'd met his match.

"Thanks again," Melody said when they'd finished up. "I'd better be heading to bed." She wiped her hands on a towel and turned to leave.

As though someone else was controlling his body, Roman's hands were suddenly on her hips. He spun her around, pulling her close against him as he pressed his lips to hers. Roman expected her to pull back and slap him. He deserved it for just grabbing her like that without permission.

Melody stiffened in surprise, stepping backward as she caught her balance, but then melted into his embrace. Her hands slid up his chest, across his shoulders, and around to the back of his neck as her lips grew pliant and welcoming.

He dared to flick his tongue into the warm depths of her mouth, exploring, needing to know more of her. Roman knew his erection from earlier in the day had returned, but he was no longer embarrassed by it. He drove it against her, wanting her to know that she wasn't just some fluke. It wasn't just that he was a lonely vet who happened to find the comfort of a woman. No, this was his mate. He didn't know what it would mean for their future, and at the moment, he didn't care. Roman tightened his grip, locking his hands around her lower back, and held her close. He would've stood there and kissed her until the sun came up, and if that's all that he could've had, then he would've gladly taken it.

But Melody had other ideas in mind. She broke

their liplock and pushed back against his chest. One hand slid down the inside of his arm to his hand, her fingers interlocking with his as she smiled up at him. Her brown eyes glittered as she turned away, pulling him along with her.

Not daring to ask questions, Roman followed. They moved through the house on bare feet, two souls who'd waited so long to meet each other. Melody could've guided him down to the pits of hell and he would have followed. But she led him up the stairs, down the hall, past the room where Amar had arranged for him to stay, and into a different bedroom. He knew it was hers without even asking, just by its scent. The white and gold accents were the same warm, inviting colors of the holiday she loved so much. Being there in her room, where she slept, where she dreamed, lit him on fire.

As soon as she closed the door behind them, Roman had her in his arms once again. He cradled the back of her skull in his hand as he kissed her hungrily, letting his tongue meld with hers as excitement shot up from his groin.

Her hands found the hem of his undershirt, and she stripped him of it, tossing it to the side as though it were completely inconsequential. Melody's eyes widened as she took in the sight of him shirtless, reaching out to touch the solid planes of his chest.

He closed his eyes to linger in the experience of her fingers on his skin, but he soon opened them again. Roman wanted to see her. She looked tempting enough in her fitted tee and pajama bottoms, but he wanted more. Slowly, carefully, he pulled her free of her clothing and reveled in every inch of her flesh, from the curve of her breasts, to the smoothness of her stomach, down to the arc of her hips and even the length of her legs. In the dim light, he found freckles to match the ones across the bridge of her nose, and he kissed every one of them. She laughed, and sometimes she moved away as his beard tickled her, but she never retreated from his arms.

The two of them tumbled to the bed together, not even bothering to pull back the covers. Melody trapped him with her legs, her knees clutched around his hips as she pulled him down toward her. She wanted him, and he wasted no time giving her what she craved. He buried himself inside her, and just the way they'd moved with such harmony in the kitchen, their hips moved with the same sense of synchrony. When he retreated, she advanced. When he pushed forward, she pulled back. Roman knew nothing of music, but he couldn't help but think of it when it came to her. She was the song to his soul, the one who knew the tune to his very being.

Roman could feel the tension build inside him, like a wire being slowly twisted. Scooping his hands around her backside, he tossed himself to the side and rolled over, pulling her on top of him. She laughed and clung to his shoulders, her curls tickling his face until she got control of herself and pushed up.

Melody arched her back as she took him in as deeply as she could. Her toes curled against the sides of his legs as she tossed her head back and braced her hands on his shoulders. She was taking what she needed from him, and Roman was ready to give it. He moved his hips in time to hers as he took her nipple into his mouth, circling it slowly with the tip of his tongue. Roman's hands clung to her ass, and she groaned with pleasure as his fingers sank deep into her flesh.

Her eyes closed and mouth slackened as her core tightened around him, inviting him to join her on the journey of pleasure she was flying on. She gripped his shoulders hard as she came, tiny gasps escaping from her throat.

Roman let himself go, and a shudder of pleasure

whipped down his back as they pushed each other ever higher. His bear's roar rose from his throat as he plunged himself yet further inside her, wanting to feel even the tiniest spasm from within her. She was his. It might only be for now, but she was his.

4

Melody woke slowly and peacefully, stretching throughout the length of her body before she even opened her eyes. She knew without looking that Roman was there next to her. She could sense him. It wasn't just his scent or the way the mattress felt different at having a second person in the bed. Her body simply *knew,* and she liked that sense of knowing. Even so, she dared to open her eyes and take a peek.

He lay on his back, his face serene. She took the time to enjoy the way his hair fell back against the pillow and how his eyelashes looked much longer when his eyes were closed. He had beautiful lips, and a small thrill shot through her stomach as she remembered what they felt and tasted like. Though perfectly relaxed, she could see the outline of every muscle in his incredible body. Melody had no idea how long he'd been out of the service, but it was clear that he still kept in shape.

Her snow leopard purred with contentment as she watched him sleep. Roman was the kind of man she could've easily just tumbled into bed with for a one-night stand. Melody was pretty sure she could've done that and not regretted it for an instant, but she still preferred the way things had actually gone. She closed her eyes once more as she relived their evening on the couch, discussing the correlations between the world of George Bailey and the current world they lived in... eating to their hearts' content... slowly moving closer to each other both physically and emotionally... It'd felt so real and so mature, like a relationship she could truly be comfortable in.

No. She couldn't call it a relationship. Roman was scheduled to go back to Wyoming once the holidays were over. He had a life up there, and she couldn't ask him to change that any more than he could ask her to leave the Force. It would never work. She'd also noted that hardness that'd taken over his face for just a fraction of a second when she'd asked if he had any children. Even if their locations weren't a problem, that part would be. Roman didn't seem to want children, and Melody couldn't see her life without them.

Furrowing her brow, she tried to concentrate only on the good parts. She did have a beautiful naked man in her bed, after all. There wasn't anything pressing on the schedule for the day, and her ears had yet to pick up on anyone else being up and out of bed. *He probably won't mind if I wake him up for a repeat of last night...*

Pushing herself up onto her elbow, she leaned across the bed to stroke his inner thigh when a baby's cry split the air.

Roman's eyes flew open, and he was up and off the pillow. "What was that?"

Melody's body had also reacted to the sound with an instinctive drive that she'd never been able to understand. It was the same feeling she had every time she was in a store and heard a child cry for its mother. It sparked a physical reaction that demanded her to help, even though she had no child of her own.

She'd bounced off the mattress and was frantically searching for her pajama bottoms. "It's just..." She was going to say it was just Lucas, ready to wake up and start the day. But Emersyn's boy had outgrown crying when he woke up. This was the sound of a younger baby, and it was coming from much further away than the nursery down the hall. "I don't know."

Roman yanked on a shirt, but it wouldn't go past his shoulders. He ripped it back off again and tossed it to her. "I think this is yours."

Melody had already put on a different one, but having found her pants, she slipped them on as well. "I'm going to check on Lucas first."

"I'll go with you." He was at her back as soon as she had her hand on the doorknob.

She had it covered and was more than capable of peeking in the baby's room, but Melody didn't argue. Something had changed in the air, and she could sense it just as she'd been able to sense Roman was at her side without seeing him. Was she simply becoming more perceptive now that her body had tapped into knowing what it was like to have a mate? There was no time to think about it.

Racing down the carpeted hallway, Melody knew before she even opened the door that it wasn't Lucas. It wasn't his cry. But who else would be making that noise? She looked in the nursery just to be safe. He was in his crib, just as he should have been. His dark hair was tousled from sleep, but his lashes lay peacefully on his cheeks. His breathing was even, and he most certainly wasn't crying. Fortunately, he hadn't been woken up by whoever was.

Melody shut the door quietly. "This is very strange," she murmured as she began moving through the house.

"No other kids live here, do they?" Roman asked.

"No, just Lucas." She headed down the stairs, realizing she was following an innate sense more than she was trusting her hearing, though she could certainly hear better than most humans. Her body moved with the litheness of her inner cat as she swept down the stairs and into the living room. The Christmas lights that had looked so welcoming the night before now only looked like clutter as she tried to figure out what was happening. "It's coming from outside."

"Hold on, I'll look." Roman reached for the door handle.

But Melody had it first. She had to see what was there. A child was crying, screaming practically, and it needed someone. It needed her. Pounding her code into the electronic lock, she flung open the front door.

The volume of the baby's wailing increased exponentially, filling the air. Melody hardly heard it as she looked down, seeing a car seat on the front porch. The handle was still up, and a yellow blanket covered the top of it. She immediately knelt and pulled the edge of it back to find the red, pinched face of a baby, screaming so hard, its tiny tongue was vibrating.

"You poor sweet thing!" Scooping up the entire carrier, Melody turned and brought the child inside.

"I didn't see anyone else out there," Roman said as he closed the door behind her.

Melody's heart swelled with sadness. "Who could leave you like that?" she gently cooed to the screaming baby. It blew her mind that something like that could still happen in this day and age, yet there the little girl was. With expert fingers, Melody deftly pulled the blanket out the rest of the way and unfastened the buckles. "She's hungry, and her diaper is more than full," she said as she lifted the squirming bundle free. Melody turned to Roman. He looked completely lost, standing there with his pajama pants on backward and his hair a rumpled mess. His eyes were wide, and he moved his hands as though he were ready to take some sort of action, but he didn't know what it was.

"Do me a favor and wake up Emersyn. There's no telling how long this poor little thing was on the porch, and she'll need to be looked over. I'm taking her into Lucas's room to get her cleaned up, then I'll be back down here to make her a bottle." Melody pulled the little girl close and headed for the stairs.

"Sure." Roman raced up ahead of her, clearly glad to have something to do.

Melody smiled as she slowly headed upstairs, pushing the tip of her finger into the baby's palm. The little girl gripped it tightly, her tiny knuckles turning white. "That's right. You go ahead and be angry. You have every right to be. How could anyone do such a terrible thing?" Turning down the hall, Melody opened the door to Lucas's room. The screaming baby might very well wake him, but they'd just have to deal with it. This child had to be taken care of.

"Here you go, sweetling," Melody cooed as she laid her out on the changing table. "I'm so sorry. I know these diapers aren't quite the right size, but they're better than nothing for now. I'll go out to the store later to get you something that fits you a little better. And some clothes, too. For right now, I think I have some clothes Lucas has grown out of. He won't mind if you borrow them." Anytime she'd dealt with little ones, she'd always chattered at them about what she was doing. She'd later read that it was good for their language development, but Melody enjoyed doing it regardless.

"Who's that?" Melody turned. Lucas was standing in his crib, gripping the side of it with one hand and pointing at the newcomer with the other. "You have a baby, Aunt Mel'dy?"

"No, it's not my baby," she admitted, though even speaking that simple truth broke her heart a little. The baby was calming down now that she had a clean diaper on, and Melody was already falling in love with her. There was just something so enchanting about babies. It was like they could reach inside and touch her heart with their tiny fingers. They were so soft and warm and sweet, the kind of qualities you didn't always find in adults.

"Who's baby 'dat?" Lucas pressed.

She couldn't blame him. He'd just woken up to find a new child in his room. But that was a very hard question to answer at the moment. "Well, she's just a baby I'm watching for a little while."

"You not gonna watch me?"

Clothed in an old onesie that sagged off her little behind, Melody lifted the girl off the changing table. She cradled her against her chest and brought her over for Lucas to see. "Of course I'll still be watching you," she assured him as she reached out to touch his shock of dark hair. "Nothing between us will change. This little girl needs my help right now, that's all."

"Name?"

Lucas had always been inquisitive. Most of the time, Melody admired that about him. She loved to see how bright and interested he was, but right now, it was making her life harder. Melody hesitated. If there had been any sort of note in the baby seat, she hadn't seen it. She'd have to go back and check. For the moment, perhaps it was best to just make something up. "Her name is..."

"Ruby," said a voice behind her.

Melody turned to find Roman standing in the doorway. He held up the yellow blanket that had been wrapped around the baby, and Melody could see there was a name embroidered on it. "Ruby," she repeated as she gazed down at the sweet little bundle. With her dusting of blonde hair and her big blue eyes that were still full of tears, having a name to attach to that precious little face just made

Melody fall for her even harder. "Such a pretty name."

"I can play with Ruby?"

"Maybe later. Right now, she needs some breakfast." And a thorough checkup. Melody hadn't noticed anything wrong with Ruby—not even a diaper rash—but she knew it was best if the doc had a look at her. "Roman, will you please help Lucas out of his crib and bring him downstairs? My arms are kind of full."

He hesitated before taking a step forward. Roman moved to the side of the boy's bed and reached in, helping him down to the floor. He let go once Lucas was on his feet, but the tot immediately reached back up. Lucas held his hand as naturally as if Roman had been his father as they headed out of the room.

Despite the strange situation she'd just found herself in, Melody smiled as she headed back down the stairs to the kitchen. Roman was a big guy, a burly soldier, the type of man who'd probably killed and saved numerous lives during his career in the service. He exuded a quiet strength that Melody admired, but she couldn't help but find it a little funny that he seemed intimidated by a toddler. Not everyone had spent their teen and college years babysitting, though.

"I know, Ruby, I know," she crooned as the baby began screaming all over again. "I think I've got a bottle in here somewhere for you." Working with one hand and holding Ruby with the other, Melody quickly flipped through the cabinets. She was grateful that Lucas had only recently stopped using a bottle and that they'd stashed them away instead of getting rid of them just yet. There was even an unopened can of formula, much to her relief. "Almost there, baby girl. Almost there."

"Melody!" Emersyn came rushing into the kitchen with her arms out. "Roman told me what happened. Unbelievable!"

The room suddenly got much quieter as Melody gave Ruby the bottle. "I know, but here she is."

"Was there a note or anything?" Emersyn asked as she began looking Ruby over.

"Nothing," Roman confirmed as he joined them, still being guided by Lucas. "Sorry. It took us a minute to get down the stairs."

Melody clamped her lips together and looked back down at Ruby. She knew Lucas still took the stairs one at a time, and she would've given anything to watch Roman have to do the same.

"I didn't find anything on or in the car seat, and I checked the front porch thoroughly," Roman continued. "Do you have any surveillance cameras set up?"

Amar joined them just then, and he, too, came over to study the little girl. "I'll have Raul check through the feeds. Anything that has to do with tech immediately goes to him." He rubbed the back of his neck. "Of all the problems we've had to solve, I never would have thought we'd be presented with one like this."

"Is it possible that someone just left her on the doorstep of a nice house in the hopes that she'd have a good life?" Melody asked. It was the kind of thing you saw in old books or movies, but not the kind of thing that happened in reality.

"We'll figure it out soon enough," Amar assured her. "Melody, can I ask you to take care of her until we do?"

"Already on it, Chief," she assured him. Melody braced the bottle as she grabbed a cloth to wipe a dribble of formula from Ruby's chin. She felt awful that this adorable creature had been taken away from her mother and left with strangers, but her heart secretly soared.

"Great. I'll get everyone together, and we'll have a

meeting in one hour." Amar strode purposefully from the room.

"I'll wait until she's done eating, then I'll take her into the exam room," Emersyn said. "She sure is a cutie."

"I'm not going to argue with that." Melody smiled down at the cherubic face. She hadn't asked for a baby for Christmas, but it looked like she was getting one anyway.

5

Roman stepped out the back door. It had been less than an hour since he and Melody had found that child on the doorstep, though it'd felt like a lifetime. The world was heaving and changing underneath him, and he couldn't do anything about it. He belonged back in Sheridan. He knew that without even a trace of doubt. It was the one place he'd found that he really belonged, and the solitude of the rural Wyoming community was good for him.

But then he'd had to come to California and meet Melody. Roman walked out past the pool, gazing into its blue depths as he recalled the night before. He'd been unable to sleep in a new place, and the temptation of all those leftovers from the party had been irresistible. He hadn't counted on finding something—or rather, *someone*—even more irresistible when he'd wandered into the kitchen. Roman smiled, remembering how she'd been swinging her ass from side to side as she sang, with hardly a care in the world. That was the beginning of all this change, but it was a change that was much easier to fall into.

He'd been so comfortable with her as they sat on the couch and watched that old movie. Roman couldn't remember a time in his life when he'd found that level of ease so quickly with someone. That was just one of the many reasons he knew Melody was his mate. He could see himself falling for her just as easily as he'd fallen into bed with her, disrupting his entire life just to be with her. He knew, though, that it wouldn't work if either of them had to give up what they loved.

That notion had been driven home as soon as he'd seen Melody dive into action with Ruby. She hadn't delayed for half a second when she'd seen that child on the front porch, nor had she shown any reluctance to take care of her simply because she wasn't biologically hers. In fact, the way Melody carried Ruby around, cooing and fussing over her, it was hard to believe she wasn't the baby's mother.

Roman shoved his hands in his pockets and tried

to appreciate the scenery of the landscaped backyard, but it was too difficult to concentrate. All he could see was the beatific look on Melody's face as she gazed at Ruby. There had been an instant connection between the two of them, and Roman wasn't sure how he felt about it. It was something akin to jealousy, but there was so much more to it. It was his own history that was affecting him, a history that was still too fresh for him to just brush off. He was crazy about Melody, but he couldn't possibly give her what she needed. He scuffed his foot in the grass. They'd already decided that it wasn't going to work out for him, and there was no point in lamenting over it now.

"Roman?" Jude stood at the back door, a cup of coffee in his hand. "The meeting's just about to start. Amar said you'd probably want to sit in on it."

"Thanks." Roman's lips began to form a protest, explaining that he wasn't part of the Force and had no reason to be at that meeting, but his feet had a different plan and began walking across the grass toward the house. "I don't want to intrude on anything, though."

Jude lowered his chin slightly, his pale eyes penetrating as he looked into Roman's. Jude had a certain sense of gravitas about him that suggested he knew far more than he said. "You're not. Any friend of Amar's is a friend of ours. Come on in, man."

Roman followed Jude inside. He'd been on some crazy missions during his time in the service. He'd done things that most civilians couldn't even imagine, yet sitting in on a meeting was making him more nervous than heading to war with a Glock 19 in his hand. That feeling was only magnified when he saw Melody step into the conference room ahead of him. It was one thing to sit in on the Force's briefing, but it was only going to be harder now that he knew Melody was there.

The conference table was a long behemoth of polished wood with comfortable chairs arranged around it. With the fresh paint and a flatscreen television on the wall, the room looked like it belonged in a corporate office building instead of the headquarters of a shifter-based team of soldiers. Roman almost thought he should be wearing a suit to attend this meeting versus his t-shirt and jeans.

Amar took his place at the head of the table. "All right. I think we all know by now what's happening, but let's run through all the facts. We've got a child in our custody, and I want to get this figured out as quickly as possible. I'm sure the parents are worried to death. Melody, let's begin with you since you were the one who found Ruby."

She sat to Amar's right with the baby on her lap, holding her as naturally as if she'd been taking care of the child from the day she was born. Melody had managed to find time to get dressed and pull her hair into a ponytail. The cinnamon curls burst from the back of her head, and several wild tendrils escaped the fastening and fell to frame her face. Roman thought her hair's unruliness was quite the contrast to the calm, organized way Melody had acted when it came to Ruby.

Lifting her eyes and glancing at him for a moment, Melody told her side of the story. "Just after I woke up, I was still lying in bed and heard a baby's cry. I knew that it couldn't have been Lucas. I mean, I've spent enough time with him that I just know. I checked his room anyway, but he was sound asleep. Then Roman and I found Ruby outside."

Roman raised a brow at this last sentence, but he merely nodded in response. "Did you see any sign of another person out there? Any indication that someone might've been watching from nearby?"

Melody's head had fallen forward to look at Ruby once again, her cheeks glowing. "Honestly, I couldn't say. I was too focused on the baby to notice."

"Roman?"

Looking to his old friend, Roman felt called out. He'd just slept with Melody right there at Force headquarters. It felt like a betrayal to Amar's clan, but he knew he wasn't being called to the carpet for that. They needed to find this child's parents, and that was the only thing that really mattered. "After Ruby was brought inside, I took a look around. I don't know your neighborhood the way you do, but I didn't see anything that looked out of the ordinary."

Amar gave another nod, and if he was upset with Roman for his nighttime activities, he gave no indication. "Right. Raul, you installed security cameras for us not too long ago. Were you able to find anything?"

The wolf shifter stood up, his cell in his hand. He used it as a controller to project several images up onto the television. "I've been through all the footage as thoroughly as I can, and I used a few software programs to enhance the images. Unfortunately, as you see here, whoever did this was very careful to disguise themselves."

Roman ripped his gaze away from Melody to study the screen. A robed figure, shown in several different still shots, came up the walkway and deposited the car seat on the porch. Whoever it was had taken great pains not only to swathe themself in thick clothing that completely disguised their figure. With the head covered as well, Roman could hardly tell if he was looking at a man or woman. "That doesn't help much."

Raul shook his head. "No, it really doesn't. I've got some pretty sophisticated facial recognition software, but I can't exactly use it if there's no face."

"What about the city cameras? Can you trace this person by tapping into those?" Amar was firing questions just as quickly as they could be answered. Roman could see why he'd been chosen as Alpha of this group, though it hadn't surprised him in the first place. He'd always acted as a natural leader out in the field.

"I tried," Raul admitted. "Our cameras indicated this person approached from the west and left that way, too. I used the time stamp and direction to patch into the appropriate city cameras. They're a little glitchy, so some of the information I have is mere inference, but there's a good possibility this person came from one of three clans." He switched the image on the screen to a map with three green dots indicating the clans' locations.

"It's so strange," Melody mused. "Why would someone leave a child on our doorstep?"

Amar leaned forward, bracing his elbows on the table. "I think we can take a safe gamble that whoever did this is a shifter, and they must know this is our headquarters. As the Force has gained more and more recognition, it's not surprising, nor is it something worth completely repressing. At least we know that someone—whoever this person is— likely came to us for help. I only wish I knew more. Emersyn, do you have any medical findings on the baby?"

Sitting next to Melody, Emersyn shook her head. "Nothing pertinent. As far as I can tell, she's a shifter. I haven't seen any signs yet as to what species. She seems to be in perfectly good health, other than she might've missed an early morning meal. Melody has already taken charge of getting her cleaned up and fed, and at this point, she's no different than any other baby."

"Yes, thank you for stepping in, Melody," Amar added. "It's very much appreciated."

"I'm more than happy to do it," Melody admitted as she contemplated Ruby once again. Her eyes were so soft, her smile so genuine. "I feel bad for her because this obviously isn't the perfect situation, but she's a complete angel."

As Melody lifted a hand to brush back Ruby's

soft, blonde hair, Roman felt another pang of regret ripple through his chest. She'd told him how she loved children, and it was obvious now that he saw her in action with a little one. He could see this wasn't just something Melody said because she thought it was expected of her as a woman. She adored that child in her arms, even though she had no ties to it. She would do anything for Ruby.

It broke his heart. Melody was his mate, and he knew that. It made him entertain ideas like finding a way for the two of them to be together, no matter where they lived. But a child? The idea thickened his throat. He couldn't do that. He couldn't be a father, not after what'd happened.

"I've scanned The Shift thoroughly, but I haven't found any posts or even hints about a missing child," Raul was saying as Roman returned his attention to the meeting.

"The Shift?" Roman asked.

"It's a news app with a social media aspect I created for shifters only," Raul explained. "With the help of the geniuses over at Taylor Communications, anyway. Shifters can only activate it if they have an access code generated by their Alpha, which would have to come from us first. It helps us build our registry of shifters in the area, plus it keeps out any prying eyes. Normally, it's a pretty good source for leads."

"The lack of information isn't comforting," Amar replied. "If someone were missing this child, I would think they'd have something to say about it. Unless, of course, something had happened to them."

"I certainly hope that last part isn't something we'll have to worry about," Jude said quietly.

"Agreed," Amar said with a nod. "Our first line of business is to track down the parents, no matter what their status is. We'll start by getting in touch with the three clans who could be tied to this incident and see if we can arrange peaceful meetings with them. In the meantime, let's keep our eyes and ears open for any other hints that might point us in the right direction, whether it's something online or in person." He hesitated, tapping his fingers on the desk. "If the parents can't be located or if we find they're dead, we'll cross that path when we come to it. You're all dismissed."

Roman made his way out of the conference room, though a few others held back to talk with Amar. He felt the urge to act building in his muscles once again, feeling as though he needed to do something to make this situation better. Unfortunately, he didn't know what that was. He also didn't know how he was going to deal with the problem of Melody.

"How's she doing?" he asked as she stepped out of the conference room behind him.

When she looked up at him, he was unsure if the kindness in her eyes was actually for him, or if it was from looking at the baby. "As well as can be expected. She's young enough that she might not know a major difference, especially if she's used to being dropped off with a sitter regularly. As long as someone's taking care of her, she should be content. Lucas was a lot like that. He still is, actually. He sees everyone here as one big family. Even though I'm technically the one who watches him, he's still just as happy as a peach as long as it's one of us. He's with Mali right now, and I'm sure it doesn't bother him a bit."

"The Force members sure are a tight-knit group," Roman observed, "even those who don't actually live here." Why did he feel a little envious of that? He had his own clan up in Sheridan. It wasn't a family he'd been born into, much like what the Force had going on there in L.A., but they were good to him.

"We really are," she agreed. "I didn't have a big family growing up, so it's great to always have someone to lean on."

He felt yet another crack form in his heart. This woman was utterly perfect. Even if she suddenly agreed to go to Wyoming with him, he'd be moving her to the middle of the wilderness where she didn't know a soul. She was strong, and while he had no doubt she'd be able to handle it, she still wouldn't be happy. "The Army was kind of like that," he said for lack of anything else. "I was closer to some than others, but you always had your brothers at your back."

"Yes, and that sense of camaraderie is thick around here," she said with a smile. She looked down as Ruby stretched and wiggled in her arms, turning her head toward Melody's chest and making tiny noises of distress. "Looks like it's time for another bottle."

He watched her head toward the kitchen, on the verge of asking if she needed any help or what he should do, but he knew there was nothing. This was Melody's life. This was her way of being, and she didn't need him to get involved. It was better if he stayed out of the picture as much as possible. The real question was how long he'd be able to do that for.

6

Emersyn let out an exasperated sigh as she rushed around the exam room at headquarters, packing up a few supplies she needed for the day. She'd swept her dark hair back into a braid, but tiny strands were already pulling free. "I'm never going to get out of here on time."

"The clinic will be there when you get there," Melody reminded her calmly as she lifted Ruby into her arms. "You worry too much."

"Maybe so," she said with a flick of her fingers in the air as she tried to remember what else she was supposed to get for the day. "It's just that every day I wake up and think I must have missed something when it comes to Ruby's health. I just feel like there should be something wrong with her if someone was going to leave her here, you know?"

"I do," Melody admitted. She'd thought about it several times herself, but every time she looked at or took care of Ruby, the little girl seemed completely fine. "It's all really strange. I guess I see this as just a different kind of babysitting job. I'll take care of her until her parents come for her, whenever that may be."

Emersyn paused in her frenzy and looked Melody in the eye. "Mel, you know it's probably not going to be the kind of thing where we get to keep her, right? I mean, even if we discover that her parents are dead, there's probably a relative who'll want her."

"Oh, I know that. Of course." Melody shifted Ruby in her arms. She hadn't admitted it to anyone, and she'd hardly been able to admit it to herself, but she would've gladly raised Ruby as her own. She didn't care if she shared blood with her or not.

"And you're sure you're going to be okay watching both Lucas and Ruby today? The two of them are going to be a handful."

Melody shook her head, setting her red curls bouncing over the shoulders of her light sweater. Several of the other women had helped out since

Ruby arrived, giving Melody time to take care of her other duties, but she was looking forward to having both of the little ones to herself. After all, that's probably how things would be from now on until they figured out what to do with Ruby. "It won't be a problem at all. I've got a big day of activities planned, including heading over to the L.A. Zoo Lights.

Emersyn lifted an eyebrow as she stowed an extra pack of syringes in her medical bag. "You're a braver woman than I am. Maybe Amar ought to have you out running missions instead of running the homestead."

"No way," Melody replied as she lightly tapped the tip of her finger against Ruby's nose. "Then I'd miss out on all the fun."

When Emersyn had gone and the rest of the Force was going about their day, Melody launched into the endless series of events revolving around caring for two little ones. She fed snacks and cleaned up after them. She mixed formula and washed bottles. The small layette she'd ordered for Ruby was delivered, and Melody delighted in washing up all the dear little outfits so she could play dress-up with the new baby. She taught Lucas to be gentle with their houseguest, and she answered his questions about her as patiently as she could. It was difficult when she knew so few of the answers, but fortunately, he was far more interested in their evening plans.

"Zoo?" he asked as he spun a wooden block in his hands, examining the colorful sides.

"No, it's not quite time to go to the zoo yet. We have to wait until it gets closer to dark." Melody stood up from the floor and stretched, wondering when she'd gotten old enough that her knees felt so terrible after sitting cross-legged on the carpet.

"Dark?" He ran to the sliding glass door and peered out.

"Yeah. How else are we going to see all the pretty Christmas lights? I think Ruby will have fun, too. Don't you?"

Lucas marched over to where Ruby sat peacefully in the bouncy seat Melody had dug out of the attic, playing with an oversized set of plastic keys. He twisted his mouth and tipped his head from side to side. "Yeah, I guess so."

"It's been a long time since we've been to the zoo, but this will be a bit different. We won't see the same kinds of animals we normally do. They'll all be asleep."

Roman happened to walk into the room just

then. "You're going to the zoo at night?"

Her heart lifted as soon as she saw him. Melody didn't want to have that reaction. She wanted to feel the same way about him as she did any other man in this household, like she was seeing someone familiar and kind but nothing more than a friend. Her body, and especially her snow leopard, didn't seem to share the same desire. "Yeah. They have a big Christmas light event at night, and I'm going to take the kids. I thought they'd have fun."

"Are you going by yourself?" He stood next to the couch with his hands on his hips as he surveyed the disaster area that the living room had become after an entire day of entertaining two children.

Melody laughed. "Since when is it impossible for one adult to leave the house with two children? I can handle them."

"I'm sure you can, but I'm not sure you should."

She didn't like the dark look that had come over his face. It was as though he were completely somewhere else in his mind. "What do you mean?"

"This is a big city, and I'm sure an event like that draws a decent crowd. Plus, you'd be out after dark by yourself, trying to find your car in the parking lot…" He trailed off as he lifted his hands in the air in turn, weighing all the possible, horrible options.

"And we don't know what Ruby's circumstances are," he added.

Though she wasn't exactly sure what he meant by that, Melody didn't mind a little company. It would be a good excuse to spend more time with Roman, which had been difficult since they'd discovered Ruby. She'd hardly talked to him at all, and though things had been amicable after their night together, she didn't want anything to feel awkward. "Sure. You can come if you want to."

When they arrived at the L.A. Zoo an hour later, Melody quickly found a place to park and hopped out of the car, heading for the trunk. She whisked out one of the strollers and opened it with a snap. "I'm so excited! I have to admit I enjoy the lights just as much as the kids do, or maybe even more so since I understand all the work that goes into them. The weather is absolutely beautiful for this!" The temperatures had dropped into the fifties, making it just cool enough to bundle up and feel the coziness of the season without having to worry about keeping the kids warm.

Roman didn't appear to be enjoying himself at all as he tried to figure out the stroller. He shook the handle as he bent over and ran his hand down the side. "Is there a button or a switch or something for this thing?"

Melody reached over. She grabbed the handle and the button next to it, and the stroller popped open with a flick of her wrist. "Don't look at me like that," she said with a laugh. "I've been doing this for a while, so I'd better be familiar with the equipment. I'll get the kids."

When she had Lucas and Ruby buckled into their respective strollers, Melody was pleased to see Roman wrap his thick fingers around the handles of Ruby's. He looked a little apprehensive, but it was clear to her now that he just didn't have much experience with kids. She couldn't knock him for that, and she certainly had to admire him for trying.

They meandered along the paved pathway as Lucas waxed ecstatic over all the sights and sounds. "Look! Lion!" he shouted, pointing at the large, illuminated decoration that stood proudly along the path. "Look, Ruby, look!" Her name came out more like 'Wooby,' and it positively melted Melody's heart.

"Good job, Lucas. That is a lion. And what's that over there?" She knelt next to the stroller and pointed, directing his eyes to a polar bear. It was a completely different experience than coming to the zoo during the day and seeing the live animals, but that was one of the things Melody loved about it.

"Bear!" Lucas squealed.

Roman smirked, leaning close to Melody as they moved on. "You know, I'd think there would be certain species he'd be less interested in seeing, considering he sees them all the time."

Melody stopped herself from leaning into Roman's warmth. Their soul-bond was hard to ignore, no matter how much logic she tried to apply to it. The night air, the bright lights, and even just seeing him watch the fascination on Ruby's face only helped cement just how incredible he was inside her heart. The man didn't know a damn thing about kids, and he was under no obligation to go there with her, yet there he was.

"You'd be surprised," she admitted. "Lucas says his favorite animal is a bear. When I ask him why, he just points to himself. I think it's kind of great that he can relate to the animal world so well, but I do have to really keep an eye on him when I bring him here during the day."

They made their way toward a canopy of trees. The mirror balls that dangled from the branches enhanced the numerous lights that surrounded them. "He gets a little too enthusiastic?" Roman asked.

Melody bit her lip, trying not to laugh. "When he was really little, he was too young for it to matter all that much. As he's gotten a little bit older and more self-aware, he's figured out who he really is at heart. Of course, living at headquarters means that he doesn't have to hold back his animal self. You combine all that, and you've got a little boy trying to jump over the railing and get as close to the real bears as he can. There was no way he could actually get to them, because of the way everything is set up here, but that didn't stop him from trying."

"Did he think he should be living with them or something?"

"You know, I think he wanted them to come home with us," Melody giggled. It was hard to keep the conversation quiet, but she didn't want Lucas to think she was making fun of him. "He couldn't really tell me because he was so upset. I can laugh about it now, but at the time, I was glad it wasn't a busy day. There weren't too many people around to see him throwing an absolute fit over not being able to take the bears home."

"That's pretty cute," Roman admitted. "I have to say, I thought these two would be too young to enjoy this, but they seem to be having a good time. Look." Roman nodded down at the little girl in the stroller.

Ruby had been swaddled in a thick knit cap and a fleece coat, and Melody had tucked a thick blanket around her in the stroller. She'd shown a good temperament so far, and even being wrapped up like the Abominable Snowbaby hadn't fazed her. She turned her head from side to side, her eyes wide as she followed all the moving, shimmering lights.

It was a sweet scene, one that Melody would be sure to gush about to Emersyn, but she found herself far more focused on Roman. The soft, colored lights bathed and softened his face. He was a handsome man in any light, but the way he looked at Ruby completely changed his features. This wasn't just a man who'd seen the suffering of war and had moved off to the Cowboy State to bury that past. This was a man who felt, who wanted to feel.

He brought out the feline side of her, and Melody wanted to rub her cheek against his shoulder affectionately. She wished she hadn't been so reserved when they'd had that time together on the couch, with the rest of the house asleep. Yes, they'd ended up in bed together, but she longed for something even more intimate. How nice it would've been to twine her fingers between his, to cuddle up against him and lean her head on his shoulder while they watched the movie, to stretch and snuggle and be completely comfortable with each other. The sex had been incredibly hot, but Melody knew it could go even deeper than that if they could get past everything else that was in their way.

"Isn't she something else?" Roman murmured, nodding at Ruby. "She must've been through a lot over the last couple of days, but she still manages to chill out and enjoy all the lights. I know she doesn't think about things the same way we do, but still. I might have a hard time if I were in her position."

The warmth in Melody's cheeks had nothing to do with the sweater she'd put on for their trip. Roman was showing her, in all the little ways, just how real of a person he was. She'd expected something different, someone more distant, when Amar had told them he was coming.

As they moved on toward the Twinkle Tunnel, Melody directed their little party over to the side. "Okay, I think it's best to stop off for some diaper changes before we get any further. I don't want to get inside that tunnel of lights and regret it." She bent down to unbuckle Lucas from his stroller.

"Um, what should I do?" Roman asked softly.

She looked up at him, seeing the sheer terror in

his face. He was trying. He'd already done a lot, considering that neither of these children was related to him biologically. "I'll just run in with Lucas, and then I'll come back to swap them out. You can stay here with the strollers if that works. Then I won't need to worry about our stuff."

Roman looked somewhat relieved, and Melody hid her smile as she took Lucas into the restroom. "Are you having fun?" she asked the little boy. The bright lights overhead were a contrast to the darkness outside, and she squinted against it.

"Yeah!" he replied enthusiastically. "More lights?"

"Oh, yes," she said as she opened the diaper bag. "Lots and lots and lots of them!"

When they emerged, she found Roman right where she'd left him. He was squatting next to Ruby's stroller, her tiny fingers wrapped around one of his as he cooed to her sweetly. Melody hated to interrupt the little tableau, and she caught the slightly self-conscious look on his face as she approached. "Ruby's turn!"

Back in the bathroom, Melody put the little blondie on the changing table and began removing all the wrappings she'd put on her to make sure she stayed warm. "I hope you're having a good time, sweetling. You are just the most adorable little thing. I know you seem to be doing okay, but I worry about you so much." She bent down and kissed her on the forehead.

Her hands deftly performed the tasks she'd become so used to over the years without thought. There wasn't anyone else in the restroom at the moment, and she quickly found herself chatting to Ruby the way she always did with babies. "You know, I can tell you this because I know you won't tattle on me, but I'm just crazy about that man who's pushing your stroller. It's too easy, when we're out here with you kids, and the weather and the lighting is all so perfect, to think that the two of us are a couple. I mean, the way I'd like us to be." She smiled as she began putting Ruby's clothes back on, grateful that the restroom wasn't too chilly for her. "I think he'd make an awfully good father himself, considering the way he pays attention to the two of you."

She was full of warm thoughts as she emerged, but her blood ran cold when she didn't see Roman or Lucas anywhere. The things he'd said at headquarters earlier about not knowing where Ruby came from or who might be after her kicked in with a shot of adrenaline, and she held the baby closer to her chest as she moved through the dim light. There were people everywhere, but she didn't see the familiar set of his shoulders.

A dark figure loomed toward her on the left, and Melody quickly turned. It was Roman, pushing both of the strollers.

"Oh, thank goodness! I didn't know where you'd gone!" she gasped as she clutched at her chest.

"Sorry. We decided to pick up some hot chocolate. Here." Roman handed her a covered paper cup.

Her fingers touched his as she took it from him. Why did he have to go and do yet another thing to make her feel this way about him? It was hard enough that their inner beasts were fighting so hard for the two of them to be together, but little things like this made it even more difficult to resist. "That was very kind of you."

"I thought it would be a nice treat," he said, his dark eyes meeting hers over the rim of his cup.

"Look! Bear!"

Melody glanced down to see that Lucas was clutching a sippy cup from the zoo's gift shop.

"They had some souvenir kids' mugs, and he went nuts for them," Roman explained. "I figured Ruby wasn't old enough for one, so I got her this." He reached under the stroller and pulled a stuffed bear with a Santa hat out of a bag.

"You're so sweet," Melody said genuinely. As they continued through the Twinkle Tunnel, made their way through a huge, lit-up storybook scene, and enjoyed a forest full of snowflakes and snowmen, Melody felt herself being lulled into a sense of family and belonging. Her snow leopard was content, gently kneading away at her heart, and almost sleepy as they reached the end of the light tour and headed for the parking lot.

"So, what did you think?" Melody asked as they pulled up next to the car and she unbuckled Ruby from her stroller.

Something about Roman had changed. His shoulders were tense, and his hands were fisted at his sides. He stood with one foot forward, as though he were ready for action. "Do you smell that?"

"Um, we *are* at a zoo," Melody joked as she opened the back door and prepared Ruby's car seat by pulling the straps out of the way.

"No, it's something else."

Just then, a figure burst out from the shadows at the edge of the parking lot. Melody turned just in time to see someone reach into the stroller and snag Ruby straight out of it. Melody screamed. She dove for the stranger, who was nothing more than a dark shape in the night. Her razor-sharp claws shot out from the tips of her fingers, her body acting instinctively, but she only snagged Ruby's blanket as it fell to the ground.

Scrambling, Melody latched onto Lucas as her mind tried to sort out what was happening. The captor turned to disappear into the trees, but Roman was after him. His feet pounded into the soft earth as he shot off into the night.

"You okay, baby?" she asked, her voice trembling as she impatiently shoved the stroller buckles aside to get to Lucas. She was terrified by what had happened to Ruby, but the important thing at the moment was to get Lucas in the car and make sure he was safe.

Pulling him up into her arms and snuggling his warm little body to her chest, Melody felt the cold metal of a knife at the back of her neck. "Give me the baby." The voice sent a shiver of horror down her spine.

It also activated her snow leopard, along with the parental instincts that Melody so rarely got to tap into, but she was in public; she had to restrain her big cat for the time being. She kept Lucas latched tightly to her torso as she punched her elbow backward, hearing the satisfying sound of air forcibly leaving the perpetrator's lungs. Immediately, Melody struck with her opposite foot before turning around and swinging a kick through the air. She didn't care where it landed, as long as this asshole understood he was not going to get away with this.

Her elbow and the first kick had made the culprit double over, so her final kick swept right across the side of his face. His head whipped to the side, and he kept the momentum going as he took off into the darkness.

"Melody!" Roman called, jogging back toward her with Ruby in his arms. The dim light showed a scratch across his face, but otherwise, he looked intact.

Tears flooded her eyes as she saw the duo. "Oh, thank God! Is she okay?"

Ruby clung to Roman, and tears shined in her big blue eyes, but Roman nodded. "Yeah. That shifter was fast, but not a great fighter. He or she gave up quickly."

Melody's hands shook as she put Lucas in the car and reached for Ruby. "Holy shit. I can't believe that. Who would do such a thing?" She would hold back as long as she could, not wanting to scare the children any more than they probably already had been, but that was just too much.

"That's the problem. We don't have any way of

knowing." Roman packed the strollers into the trunk, shut it with a slam, and took the driver's seat.

It was her car, but she didn't feel like arguing. She didn't care about the logistics, as long as they got back to headquarters. "I guess not."

Roman's hands clung tightly to the steering wheel as he backed out of their parking space. "This is exactly what I was talking about, Melody. For whatever reason that Ruby is on our doorstep, it's possible that she and anyone else around her are in great danger. You can't just go running off through the city without a care in the world."

She'd been ready to sink into the passenger seat and just close her eyes until they got home, but she straightened and turned to face him. "Excuse me?"

"You heard me. You need to be more careful. Something horrible could've happened just then. You need to call Amar and tell him about this."

"Since when are you in charge of anything?" she challenged, her adrenaline quickly funneling away from fear and toward anger. "You've been in town all a few days, and you think you can just order me around? Like I'm some idiot who doesn't know how to watch out for children?"

"Don't get all defensive on me. Amar needs to know about this. I smelled those guys, and I knew they were shifters. This obviously has something to do with Ruby." He pounded his fist into his thigh.

"Of course, but do you seriously think I need you to tell me that? Or to come down on me like I'm some sort of dumbass who doesn't understand all the possibilities? I might not be an official part of the Force, but I'm sure as shit going to do everything I can to protect these kids!" She slapped her hand over her mouth, realizing she'd cussed twice in front of the little ones now. Turning, she was relieved to see Lucas asleep in his car seat.

"Yes, you are going to do just that by staying home and keeping them as far out of harm's way as possible. I wouldn't be able to forgive myself if something happened to them." He triggered the turn signal with an angry flick of his hand.

"You?" she spluttered, unable to fathom how or why he'd suddenly come to decide that Lucas and Ruby were his responsibility instead of hers. If it had just been the two of them in the car, she would've ripped him up one side and down the other, telling him to take his polar bear ass straight back to Wyoming where he belonged. But the children were asleep, and they'd had a traumatic enough evening without seeing two grown adults fighting like children.

Instead, she crossed her arms in front of her chest and turned her head toward the window, though she hardly saw any of the lights or decorations of the city as they made their way back. As angry as she was, she could at least be grateful that Lucas and Ruby were safe. And that Roman wouldn't be joining the Force.

7
―――

"I'm not going to push you into participating, but I'm glad we've got a mission happening while you're here. It's a good chance for you to see what things are really like for us." Amar smiled, looking completely at ease behind the wheel of his sedan as they pulled onto the highway.

As much as it had felt like Christmas the night before, with the lights, festivities, and hot chocolate, the brilliant morning light and the palm trees made Roman feel like he was on a tropical vacation. He wasn't particularly in the mood for one, though. "Yeah. That's true."

"It should be a pretty easy operation today. The Alpha of this clan isn't exactly known for his pleasant disposition, nor for cooperating with other clans in the area, but he agreed to the meeting readily enough," Amar continued. "We'll just sit down with him, have a chat, and see what he has to say. Of course, you'll still want to be ready in case shit goes sideways."

"I always am," Roman said with a half-smile.

"What's eating you?" Amar asked after a moment of silence. "You've been a bit off ever since you and Melody got back home last night."

Roman let out a long breath. Ever since he'd arrived, he'd been trying to decide how to talk to Amar about this, but he'd have to do it eventually. "I know Melody is my mate."

His friend let out a light laugh. "I had a feeling. The air practically crackles between the two of you."

"Yeah, well, it doesn't anymore. She got so pissed at me last night." It was impossible to avoid each other, even in that huge house, so he'd seen her at breakfast. She'd turned away from him with a stiff jaw as she made a bottle for Ruby, and not a single word had been exchanged. "I don't understand it."

"What did you do?" Amar pressed.

"What do you mean, what did I do?" Roman's muscles bunched in his shoulders. "Why do you think it's my fault?"

Amar shrugged as he changed lanes. "Because

you're a man, and us men are usually the ones doing stupid things, as far as women are concerned. You got Ruby back, but what else did you do?"

Roman flicked his fingers in the air. "Nothing, man. I just told her she needed to be more careful, and that until we got this figured out, she and the kids needed to stay at headquarters. I told her to call you, and since I was the one driving, that only made sense."

"Hold on," Amar said, putting his hand up. "You've already hit the nail on the head. You told her she has to stay home?"

"Well, she does! It's not safe to have those kids out in public, not if someone could be after Ruby. She's got to be more careful." How could Melody not see that?

His friend pressed his lips together and sighed. "While there's certainly some sense in what you're saying, I have a feeling you said it in the wrong way. You know, the kind of way that suggests she's weak and can't fend for herself."

"But she's not," Roman countered. "I saw her take down the second attacker, all while having a kid in her arms. She definitely stood her ground." His fight with the first assailant had been easy, and he'd witnessed Melody making quick work of the second one as he came back to the car. The fire and determination inside her were easy to see, even in the darkness. It was admirable, even a little sexy.

"But you made her believe you felt the opposite," Amar pointed out.

"It scared the hell out of me to know I hadn't been right there for her when she'd needed me the most," he admitted. "I thought it was supposed to be so easy and natural when you found your mate, like everything else in the world just fell into place, and you lived happily ever after. Of course, I'd been dumb enough to think I'd found a happy ending before. I guess I'm just a fucking sucker." He braced his hand on his forehead.

"Don't be so hard on yourself. What Elizabeth did to you was wrong; there's no doubt about that. You're allowed to take time to deal with it, and you're even allowed to be mad, but you can't let it dictate the rest of your life." Amar glanced at Roman before returning his eyes to the road. "Trust me, man. I knew Katalin was the one, but when I spent all those years searching endlessly for her, it made me a shell of a man. After all those centuries, I was lucky enough to find her somehow, but I still have to wonder how different my life might've been if I hadn't let the trauma of losing her get to me."

Roman wanted to argue, simply because he was angry about how much he'd screwed up everything with Melody. He'd hated seeing the way she'd dismissed him once they'd gotten through briefing the others the night before. A close call like that should've brought them closer together instead of further apart. They should've spent the night in bed together, holding each other and talking about how grateful they were to be all right. It didn't matter that they'd already dismissed the idea of any sort of real future as a couple. The coldness with which she'd turned away from him that morning in the kitchen was enough to haunt him until the end of his days.

He sighed. "That's easy for you to say since you were able to find her again and be together. It's not going to be like that with Melody. Even if it were, I can't give her what she really wants."

"Which is?"

"Children." She'd told him that, but Roman had seen it for himself in a way that was absolutely undeniable. Melody didn't just want to be a mother, she *needed* it.

"Ah. And so we're right back to Elizabeth once again, aren't we?"

Another sigh. How could Roman just let go of everything he'd been through? It hadn't been easy to have a steady girlfriend when he was in the service and overseas. Roman came back as often as he could, though, and even when doubts about long-distance relationships crept into his mind, Elizabeth always found a way to assuage them.

Then there'd come the moment she told him she was pregnant. Roman had been over the moon at the news. He'd been getting close to his discharge date, and this would've been the perfect way to start his new life as a civilian. He was daydreaming about all the things he would teach his son any time he wasn't on duty.

"She absolutely killed me inside," he said into the silence that had fallen between them. "My father had spent a lot of time with me growing up. He taught me how to fish, hold a gun, open a door for a lady...all that guy stuff. I soaked up everything I could from him, and he was my hero. I can't tell you how badly I wanted to be that for my son, too. I was going to be there for him, and I was going to be the good father that so many kids don't get to have. I felt awful about not being able to be home for the birth, but I told myself it would be all right because as soon as I was out of the service, I'd be there all the time. Every damn second."

"I know." Amar patted him on the shoulder. "I'm really sorry, man."

"Don't be. It's my own dumb fault for believing her. We had a few mutual friends who'd tried to warn me about her in the beginning, but I was too in love to listen. What gets me the most is I was stupid enough to fall for it." He gritted his teeth, still clearly remembering how his heart had soared at seeing little Aiden on video calls from Elizabeth. Roman had thought he was the most precious thing in the world, and his love for the baby surpassed even what he'd felt for Elizabeth. Without having even met him in person, Roman had dedicated his entire being to this child. And then he'd gone home for the last time.

He'd been so nervous, even though he'd told himself how stupid that was. Aiden was a baby, and he wouldn't have any idea how significant of a meeting he was about to have. It would be the start of the rest of their lives together, and the time Aiden had spent without his father would simply be something they reminisced about over the dining table in the future.

But Roman had known right away that Aiden wasn't his. He could smell it on him. This was some other man's kid. Elizabeth had denied it, of course, and she'd even thrown it back in his face. She'd lambasted him for being irresponsible enough to have a child when he couldn't even be stateside for Aiden's birth, as though it hadn't been her fault, too. Finally, when he'd insisted on a DNA test to prove it, she'd caved.

"So much for my life as a family man," Roman continued. "I was so angry and so hurt, but more than anything, the emotional scars left me jaded about ever being a father. All that hope, all that joy, everything I'd built out in my head about raising a son... just to be gone like that in a matter of seconds? Man, I just can't deal with that kind of pain. Not now, not ever. How can I possibly try to continue things with Melody when I know she could never really be happy with me?"

Amar tapped his fingers on the steering wheel. "You want my opinion?"

"You're going to give it to me, anyway."

"You're damn right I am."

Roman ran a hand over his head. "I guess you're going to tell me not to let the past get in the way, but I don't see any way around it. I've already messed up as it is by exploding on Melody at the zoo. It's better if she thinks I'm an asshole."

"Do what you want, but you can't escape fate.

Whatever is meant to happen will happen." Amar flicked on his turn signal and veered onto the exit ramp.

"Yeah, speaking of that, there's something we need to talk about." He rubbed a finger alongside his nose, unsure of exactly how to broach this. "I don't want to upset you as Alpha of the house, but Melody and I slept together." Roman braced for a possible detonation from Amar. He didn't want to disrespect the Alpha, nor his housemates. Roman was trusted as a guest, and he couldn't have kept his dick in his pants for even the first 24 hours?

But the other man shrugged. "I know how strong our inner beasts are, and there's no denying that the two of you have some sort of connection. These things happen. Besides, I have a feeling Melody would kick your ass if you tried anything she didn't approve of."

Roman grinned despite himself. He wanted to feel moody and dark, and maybe even a little sorry for himself, but the way Melody had defended herself and Lucas at the zoo had been incredible. Without shifting, she'd still managed to transform into a kickass fighting machine. Melody had gone from the sweet, happy woman he'd curled up and watched a movie with into a protective mother who'd stop at nothing to keep the child in her arms away from her assailants.

"Here we are," Amar announced, pulling Roman back into the present moment. They stepped out of the car and wound through the heavily landscaped walkway toward the front porch of a two-story home. Amar tipped his head back to examine it. "It always interests me to see the different ways clans live. This one seems to have a bit of funding, but they're not over the top like some of the others I've seen. At least they're not living in poverty, which is always a problem."

"I guess we can safely assume, just like our time in the service, that whether you're dealing with rich or poor, it's just as likely that someone's up to no good."

"You bet."

Roman was excited to go in and get this done. Though he had no intention of joining the Force, he needed something to keep his mind off Melody. Unfortunately, the Alpha of this clan had very little to say.

"I appreciate that you've taken the time and effort to come all the way out here," Mr. Morefield said with mock sympathy as he puffed on a cigar behind his desk. "I mean, this must be a major event if the SOS Force is involved. I can't, however, give you any clue as to what's going on in the case of this child. We prefer to keep to ourselves as much as possible. It's the much safer way to run a clan, as I'm sure you can agree."

Amar nodded. "And you're sure you haven't heard anything about either a missing or a found shifter child?" He'd been careful not to give any specific information as to where Ruby was, and he hadn't even spoken her name.

"All I can tell you is that we're all present and accounted for. I'll be sure to contact you if I find myself in need of your assistance." With a wave of his arm, they were dismissed.

"He's lying," Roman said through gritted teeth as soon as they were out the front door. "The bastards who attacked us at the zoo had a very distinct scent, and I picked up on it here. These guys are definitely involved."

"We haven't had any trouble out of this clan just yet, but I've heard a few rumors that they might not always operate on the up-and-up. Their territory butts right up next to another clan's, which is bound to cause some trouble eventually if it hasn't already."

They ducked through an arbor overgrown with vines and rounded the edge of a flower bed, where a woman was on her hands and knees working the soil. "He's lying to you," she said quietly.

"Ma'am?" Roman stopped.

She glanced behind her, toward the house, but she was shielded from view by a large bush. "Don't look down here! If they see you talking to me, I'll be in more trouble than I even want to think about." She clutched her hands in the rich soil.

Roman and Amar played along, turning to look at each other so it would look to anyone else as though they were standing on the sidewalk and having a conversation. "What do you know?" Roman asked.

"They took the child," she whimpered, a tear dripping off her jawline and into the dirt. "They didn't say anything about it, and I'm not privy to Mr. Morefield's scheme, but I heard it crying in the night. I knew it wasn't ours, and I couldn't bear the idea of it being taken away from its parents."

"So, you were the one who left her on our doorstep?" Amar asked, glancing down the block.

"No. I couldn't get away, but I sent someone who could. I would've done it myself if I could have. As it is, I may be killed just for talking to you." She wept harder, her dirty hands on her knees now.

"You can come with us," Amar offered. "We can

give you shelter until this whole thing is over with. Our vehicle is just over there, and we could be there in just a few seconds."

She shook her head emphatically. "I can't. I have obligations here. I had to tell you. As a mother myself, I had to do what I could. It wasn't even safe to risk giving the baby back to its own clan, but I believe it belongs to the one to the east of here. Please, just go before it creates more trouble for all of us."

The two men moved on to the vehicle, but as Roman climbed into the passenger seat, he couldn't help but think of Melody. This woman had gone against her Alpha at the risk of her own life because she knew how Ruby's parents must have felt. She had no obligation to Ruby's parents when it came to clan or blood, and Ruby's clan might very well have been their mortal enemies, but none of that mattered. It was just like Melody, who cared so much for children who weren't of her own womb. That was a deep kind of love that couldn't be denied.

8

"Eggs?" Lucas asked eagerly from his chair at the breakfast table.

"You want more?" Melody asked as she scooped a bit onto his plate. "You've got a good appetite this morning."

Lucas pointed at Ruby in her highchair. "Eggs, Ruby?"

"Yes, she might like some, too." It was hard to know what Ruby was used to eating, but Melody followed her instincts as best as possible. She put a spoonful of scrambled eggs onto the tray and watched as Ruby scooped them up in her fingers. The baby dropped more of them onto herself than into her mouth, but she gave a coo of pleasure as she ate.

"She likes eggs!" Lucas said triumphantly.

It was adorable, but Melody was having a hard time throwing herself into the typically happy work of childcare. As she served juice and milk and wiped up spills, she couldn't help but think about what a royal prick Roman had been. She didn't care about his past with the military. It didn't give him the right to make her feel as though she were too incompetent to take care of these children. She'd certainly kept Lucas out of harm's way, hadn't she? Hell, the whole incident might not have even happened if Roman hadn't been there in the first place. She would've known she was there on her own at night, and she wouldn't have let her guard down for a second. She had always been vigilant, even before there was any known threat.

"Mel'dy mad?" Lucas asked, scraping the last of the eggs from his plate.

She swiped a hand over her forehead, where she could feel tension building, and she forced a smile. "No, sweetie. I was just thinking about some things. Are you all done?"

He nodded eagerly, and she wiped him down and helped him out of his chair.

"Am I too late for breakfast?" Roman said as he walked into the room.

Her muscles jolted with electricity at his presence, but she quickly reminded herself that she was angry with him. Furious. She didn't want to have anything to do with him, no matter what her snow leopard said. "I thought you left hours ago."

"I did. I went with Amar to talk to a few more people. He's determined not to take any action with Ruby until we can be absolutely certain that we're putting her back in the correct arms." He grabbed a granola bar from the basket on the counter.

"That's good." Melody took a warm, damp washcloth to Ruby's face. The little girl laughed as it tickled her. Melody didn't want to smile back, because she was so damn angry, but Ruby was irresistible. At least she had her back to Roman as she returned the baby's smile. "It's important to keep her safe."

He let out a sigh as he unwrapped the granola bar that she wasn't sure how to interpret. "We think we've got a good lead on finding her parents, so it's quite possible she'll be going back to them soon."

"That's..." Melody hesitated. She knew that Ruby going home was the right thing. If this were her child, she'd certainly want her back. That was part of the problem, though. Melody had built a bond with Ruby in the short time she'd been watching her.

She'd taken her in as though she were simply part of the family, and she'd continue to care for her as long as needed. "That's good," she finally said.

"Melody, I think we should talk."

She was purposely not looking at him. She didn't want to see his handsome face and get weak in the knees all over again. Melody had every right to be angry with him, and she needed to hold onto that as much as possible. That anger would fuel her strength against the demands of her snow leopard, who apparently wasn't nearly as insulted by his comments after they'd left the zoo. Even as her human side focused on its fury, her animal side longed to sidle up next to him. Melody wished she could squirt it with a spray bottle like a naughty housecat. "I don't think we really have much to talk about."

There was no response, and when she still didn't hear anything from him after she finished washing out Ruby's bottle, she turned and expected him to be gone. Instead, he stood there leaning against the pantry, his uneaten granola bar still in his hand as he looked at her. She couldn't quite read his eyes. Was he pissed? Apologetic? Hoping to wait her out until she started talking first? That last one only made her angrier, and she cared even less about what his motives were. "What?" she demanded.

"I just...I just don't think you quite understand what happened last night."

Her lashes fluttered as she blinked several times, shocked at what he was saying. "Really, Roman? You've already insulted me once. Are you calling me stupid now?"

"Outside?" Lucas asked, pointing at the back door.

Leave it to him to de-escalate the situation. "Yes, we can go outside. Let's get our jackets on." Good, this would be the perfect chance for her to avoid any further encounters with Roman.

But Lucas had other ideas. "You play?" he asked Roman. "Outside?"

Shit. Lucas was a sweet little thing. He'd already been thinking of Roman as just another part of the family, and the trip to the zoo had only reinforced that.

"Oh, you want me to play?" Roman asked Lucas.

"Yeah! Play!" Lucas flung his hands in the air and waved them around.

Roman lifted his gaze to meet hers. "Only if it's all right with Melody."

It wasn't as though she could say no. What kind

of example would that set for Lucas? It was bad enough she was already arguing in front of him. "If you'd like," she said as coldly as possible.

With jackets on, they headed into the back yard. As soon as Lucas's little feet touched the grass, he shifted into the grizzly bear form he'd inherited from his father.

"That was quick," Roman remarked.

Melody spread out a blanket and set Ruby on it. "He was a slow start, and he didn't show any signs of his animal form until his first birthday. Once he figured it out, though, he wanted to do it all the time. We had to work with him a lot just to get him to understand that there are only certain times when it's acceptable."

Roman gestured to the tall fences that surrounded the backyard. They were mostly covered in ivy, making them even better barriers against private eyes. "Was all this already here?"

Melody flicked the tip of her tongue against the back of her teeth. She didn't want to explain anything to him. Nothing that happened there at headquarters was his business, especially if he thought he could butt in and just take over whenever he wanted. Still, they had an adorable little cub wandering around the yard, listening whether he meant to or not with the acute hearing of a wild animal. "There was a fence, but we decided to put in something that would keep us a little more secluded from the rest of the world."

The young cub stomped up to Roman and nudged him on the leg before taking off across the yard.

"What's that about?"

One of these days, when Lucas was much older, she would tell him the story of how he picked the one person she was absolutely furious with and begged him to play. "He wants you to play tag with him. He likes to do it in his bear form so he can run on all four legs instead of just two. You don't have to do it if you don't want to, though."

Roman gave her a challenging look before a shiver ran up his back and racked his shoulders. His skin exploded in white fur as he bent forward, his spine lengthening. His fingers thickened as his hands and feet turned to four huge paws. His face had stretched and molded to accommodate his animal form, and Melody soon found herself staring at a polar bear.

She'd known what he was, but it was entirely different to see his arctic beast standing in their Southern California backyard. Melody lived in a house full of shifters of all kinds. She should be used to seeing their animal forms emerge. Why did it feel so different to see Roman?

He was huge, first of all. His muscles rippled under that thick coat of fur, and even though his natural insulation had to be suffocatingly hot in this environment, he romped off across the yard after Lucas. Melody put her hand in front of her mouth as she watched them, not wanting Roman to have any idea how much she loved seeing him like this. It wasn't just the appeal of him, though she certainly had to admire his glossy coat and dark eyes that still carried a reflection of the man she'd come to know. It was also in the way he played with Lucas, how he dodged first one way and then the other as they stormed through the yard in a far more raucous game of tag than Melody ever normally played with Lucas. Roman knew little about caring for children's most basic needs, but he certainly knew how to entertain them.

She was distracted from her admiration by movement at her feet. Ruby sat on the blanket, her little fingers braced on the fabric as she watched the action in the backyard. She chattered at Lucas and Roman, blowing raspberries at them every time they ran past. She rocked back and forth on her backside.

"They're having a lot of fun, aren't they?" she said, smiling once again at how absolutely adorable this little person was. Roman had said they had a lead on her parents. Did they know she was safe? Did they have any clue their dear baby was being taken care of? Roman hadn't given her any details about the parents. What if they didn't want her at all?

Ruby thrust herself forward and caught herself on her arms. Melody bent down to make sure she was all right, but then she noticed the thin coat of hair on Ruby's ears that hadn't been there earlier that morning. Before her very eyes, those tiny ears continued to transform as they shifted up the side of Ruby's head. Her tiny baby fingernails that were only paper-thin in her human form emerged as thick black claws. The next thing Melody knew, Ruby was toddling in pure bear cub form across the grass.

"Good job, little girl!" Melody cheered.

Lucas and Roman turned to look, slowing down as Ruby meandered across the lawn to them. Lucas gamboled up to her and nudged her with his nose, while Roman was suddenly very careful about the exact placement of his paws.

Melody refused to hide her delight this time, and for the first time in the past day, she and her snow leopard were in agreement. She called her own arctic beast to the surface, and though her body had to compact itself for this transformation, it was incredibly freeing. Melody twisted and stretched as she melted down to her feline form, extending her claws as soon as she had them to grip the cool grass underneath her. There was a certain balance that came from having a long tail that complemented her body perfectly, making her feel far more comfortable in this form than as a human. Even her wild, unruly hair that she always sought to tame when she stood on two feet was no longer a problem. The silvery-white fur was warm and fluffy, its spots and rosettes acting as both decoration and camouflage.

With a flick of her tail, Melody trotted off across the yard to join the others. She stuck close by Ruby, wanting to make sure the little one was all right. The baby often lost her balance and rolled over onto her side, but she didn't seem to mind as she grabbed at her toes and rubbed her muzzle in the grass. Lucas charged at Roman from the other side of the yard, slamming into the side of the big white bear. Roman responded with a rather dramatic fall to the side, allowing Lucas to climb on top of his defeated enemy and make a tiny roar of victory. Ruby decided to join in on the triumph, frolicking over to nip at Roman's toes.

Melody watched with interest. Any man who was that thoughtful and sweet when it came to children couldn't really be as much of a jerk as she thought he was, could he? And he'd made the effort of buying both Lucas and Ruby souvenirs at the zoo. Why, then, did he always seem so hesitant when it came to kids? And why did he have to be so rude to her?

Lucas rolled off Roman and tried to engage Ruby in a new game of tag. As the two of them worked out the best way for young shifters to act like bears, Roman's dark eyes met Melody's. While in their human forms, their animals had been reaching out to each other. Now, it was her mind that reached out toward his like a curling wisp of magic in the December air, something so intrinsic and natural that Melody hardly even knew what it was as it was happening. But it persisted nonetheless, yearning toward its one goal.

Roman got up and strode away from the cubs, his body changing as he moved toward the back door. His snowy fur melted away as his ears returned to their human shape, and he straightened up onto two feet as his paws once again became fingers. That strand of something that had reached out so desperately, so instinctively for him slammed into a wall as he became a human again, just in time to open the back door and disappear.

The cubs looked disappointedly after him. Melody did, too, but she couldn't dwell on that. The most important thing at the moment was the children, not some man who couldn't seem to make up his mind about where or who he wanted to be. She swiveled her head, looking for something to distract them from having lost their playmate, and found a late-season flower growing along the fence line. Melody pounced toward it and purposely missed, leaving it bobbing and weaving in her wake. Lucas and Ruby batted at it joyfully.

Out of the corner of her eye, Melody watched the house. She wanted to give him the benefit of the doubt, that perhaps he'd realized he had something he needed to do with Amar for the mission or that he'd eaten some leftovers that'd been in the fridge too long. But Roman had given no explanation when he went inside, nor was there any sign of him returning. Whatever his problem was, she wasn't going to find out anytime soon.

9

Roman shut the door behind him and curled his hands into fists, digging his fingernails into his palms. All he'd wanted to do was talk to Melody a little and make her realize that he hadn't meant to offend her. He wasn't about to make up with her, not in the way that mates would if they were going to make their connection a permanent one. There was just something about her being angry with him that he couldn't stand, and he'd wanted to fix it. Roman wouldn't be staying there in L.A., but he didn't want to go on with the rest of his life knowing she thought of him as an asshole.

Then the kids had gotten involved. At first, Roman thought that might make it easier. They might soften Melody up a bit, make her more willing to listen to him. She didn't have to change her mind about him completely, she only had to know that he hadn't meant to hurt her feelings. The conversation Roman had wanted had been lost in the playtime of the backyard, and before Roman knew it, he was far too busy wrestling on the grass with the cubs to think about anything else.

Other than how striking Melody was in her true form. He wasn't sure he'd ever seen a snow leopard shifter before. They weren't nearly as common as the typical bears, tigers, and wolves. Though even his own form wasn't the most common, he knew it was nothing compared to the magnificence of Melody. Her feline was lithe and quick, sidestepping without a hint of hesitation to nudge Ruby when she got off balance. She happily twitched her tail in the air to create a plaything for the children, who seemed to get quite the kick out of chasing her. At one point, Melody pretended to stalk Lucas and Ruby from behind a bush, digging her paws into the grass and wiggling her hind end in the air. That had certainly caught Roman's attention, but the children were far more intrigued when she sprang out at them and dodged to the side as though she'd missed.

But then that little nudge had shown up in the back of his mind. Roman had recognized it instantly. Shifters of the same clan shared a telepathic link, one that allowed them to communicate with each other when in their animal forms. He had the same thing with his clan in Wyoming, and it was what made a clan truly feel like a family. Roman had always heard the stories of fated mates who experienced the same thing and how their bond formed that connection just like blood ties did. For the longest time, he hadn't been sure it was real. After all, he hadn't experienced that with Elizabeth. Roman had spent a lot of time convincing himself that it was little more than a fairy tale. Just as humans fantasized about romantic stories they saw on television or in the movies, shifters got caught up on some arcane notion of a particularly special bond. It was ridiculous.

Until he'd felt it coming from Melody. Roman stomped up the stairs toward his room, wishing he hadn't felt it. It was only just the softest prompt from her mind to his, something as quiet as a whisper. He'd brushed it off, choosing instead to focus on playing with the children. They were just having a good time out in the sunshine, and Roman had to be imagining things. That signal suddenly became stronger, poking a little deeper into his mind and demanding to be noticed. That was when Roman knew he had to stop it right away.

"What's eating you?" Amar asked.

Roman had hoped to avoid running into anyone else, but Amar was standing at one of the large windows that overlooked the backyard. "Why do you think anything's eating me?"

One corner of Amar's mouth lifted in a smile. "You don't really think you can fool me, do you? I've known you for too long, and I've been around shifters for too long. I doubt you fooled Melody, either, storming off in a huff like that."

"I'm not in a huff," Roman countered, though simply saying it only made him sound all the more like he was. "And why are you spying on us, anyway?"

"Me?" Amar asked innocently. "I was on my way to contact that other clan and hopefully locate Ruby's parents, and I simply stopped to watch some of my household having one heck of a good time in the backyard. That is, until you put the kibosh on it." He folded his arms in front of his chest and watched Roman expectantly.

Looking out into the yard, Roman watched as the cubs toddled after a late-season butterfly. Melody moved along behind them, stealthy and serene, with only an occasional flick of her tail. "I couldn't lead her on any longer. I allowed myself to just get lost in what was happening. It's so natural when I'm around her. But then I felt her start to get into my head. If I let that happen, then it's going to be a lot harder to turn around and head back to Wyoming when the holiday is over."

"I see," Amar said, one eyebrow raised. "I can understand, to a degree. The telepathic link is a big step, but it's also quite the confirmation of just what the two of you have going on. If you ask me—what the hell?"

He'd been looking out the window, and Roman turned to see what had caught his attention. Two large streaks of fur were bolting into the back yard, right toward Melody and the kids. Roman's inner polar bear let out a mighty roar at the mere thought of his mate and these children being in danger. It was his job—whether he wanted to admit it or not—to keep them safe, and he'd abandoned his post.

"Let's go!" Amar flew down the stairs, transforming as he moved. His deep umber skin broke apart into pieces, flipping and resettling on his body in the form of onyx scales. His spine elongated into a tail, and it whipped angrily against the floor. His face completely changed into his dragon's, complete with piercing teeth and a row of spikes on top of his head, and smoke curled from his snout. He saved his wings until he got out the door, the obsidian absorbing the sunlight. It was a sight Roman had only seen once or twice, given how much of their time in the military had to be spent as humans.

Roman was on his heels, back into his bear form as soon as his paws touched the concrete of the back patio. Adrenaline raced through his system and his lungs opened, allowing him to take in and assess even the faintest of scents in the air. He sensed the same one he'd noted before, both at the zoo and when he and Amar had gone to talk to Mr. Morefield. The bastards were back, and they were after Ruby. The only difference was that they felt safe enough to shift within the confines of the backyard, and that meant they were a far more formidable enemy than they'd been while out in public.

The two incoming enemies were bears, and with that same fetid stench coming off of them, Roman was sure they were the enemy. They were giant, with long black claws that churned up the soil as they ran, their heavy coats rolling on their backs. Their mouths gaped open, showing their teeth and the long strings of saliva that dripped from them as they anticipated the fight and their supposed victory.

Melody had noticed the threat, and she stood with her back to the children. Her ears were laid back flat against her head as she hissed, a row of fur raised all down her spine. Her yowls and hisses twisted through the air, reminding these two attackers of just who they were dealing with. Ruby sat near the fence, looking completely puzzled as Lucas stood up in front of her. He put his paws in the air and tried to look as ferocious as possible as the first assailant charged at them.

Roman closed the distance between the house and the fray, Amar in the air at his side. They wouldn't get there in time. These bears who'd intruded headquarters were after the things he wanted to protect most in the world, and even as he tried his best, he couldn't do anything to protect them. *I'm coming, Melody. I'm coming.*

He didn't know whether she heard him or not, but she wasn't going to just stand down and let the bears take Ruby. She leaped into the air as the first bear approached, sailing past his mouth and landing directly on top of his head. Her cries of anger shot through the air as her claws shredded his thick hide. Blood splattered on the grass below as she tore through his fur and skin, glistening bright and red. The bear let out a moan, but it was one of frustration as he whipped his head around and sought purchase on her. Sinking her teeth into his hide, Melody held on as the bear whipped his body from side to side, trying to shake her off like a bull rider at a rodeo. Melody sank her claws in once again as the bear's fur darkened, stained by his blood.

The second bear dodged past Melody and his comrade to get to the children, but Roman dove in front of him, forming a wall between the attacker and the little ones. Amar swept in, sending down a stream of fire, and the air filled with the acrid scent of burning fur as the bear roared his pain. Digging his claws into the grass, Roman built as much traction as possible before he barreled across the short distance. The enemy was distracted by the massive black dragon overhead, his chin turned up, leaving his throat vulnerable. There were times in war when a soldier did his best to give the foe a chance to run away or surrender, when the noblest thing was simply to stop the situation from escalating instead of slaughtering the enemy. This was not one of them. These assholes had already come after his mate once. Now he was reliving the nightmare all over again, and he'd be damned if it happened a third time.

Roman went straight for its throat, and the other

bear reared back, but it was too late. Roman's teeth sank into its flesh, clamping his jaws together as he twisted, pulling backward and taking a chunk of the other bear with him. Blood spewed over Roman's white coat, tinting it pink as he went back in again and again, his mouth filling with blood as his teeth chopped and tore. A deep bellow of fear, pain, and anguish echoed through the air, and Roman realized it was coming from his enemy. He was absolutely mad with fury as he attacked, ripping and tearing, putting all his anger and frustration into it.

A clawed hand rested heavily on his shoulder. Roman turned to attack it as well, but the red that had clouded his vision cleared just in time for him to realize it was Amar. The dragon dissolved back into his human form, folding his wings into his back and standing up straight. His face was solemn. "It's over, Roman. The children are safe." He moved toward the fence, where the two cubs were shivering against the foliage, and scooped them into his arms.

Melody! Roman turned to see Melody lying on the ground. The bear's carcass next to her was proof of the effort she'd put into the fight, but the blood that rimmed the bear's mouth showed that he'd fought back before she'd killed him. Her silvery fur was contaminated with the blood of her enemy, staining it a dingy red around her paws and mouth. The parallel slashes from the bear's claws seeped fresher blood in a brilliant crimson that made him sick to his stomach.

Slowly, tenderly, Roman began licking her wounds. His heart wrenched seeing her lying there like that on the grass, panting and shivering. The light hadn't gone out of her eyes, though, and the wounds appeared to be superficial. Shifters healed far faster than humans did, and he had no doubt she would recover. That didn't make it any easier to see her like this.

Damn it! How could he have let this happen? He'd insisted on accompanying her to the zoo because he wanted to protect her. He'd even been enough of an asshole to insinuate that she couldn't protect the children herself outside of headquarters. This fight had certainly proven that Melody knew how to hold her own, and that no place was truly safe.

"We need to get her inside," Amar said. Since Roman had arrived, Amar had mostly spoken to him as a friend, but now, he spoke as an Alpha. His orders were ones to be followed, not questioned in any manner. "I'm taking the children inside. You stay here with her, and I'll send someone out to help you carry her in."

As the dragon headed for the house, Roman sucked in a staggered breath and let his polar bear go. His muscles, strength, and size could only do so much. He also couldn't risk reaching for that link that they'd both tried to use now. "I've let you down," he said to the snow leopard as he gently scooped his hands underneath her warm body. "I can't tell you how sorry I am, Melody."

She lifted her head slightly, her eyes closing in pain as he pulled her into his arms. Roman wasn't going to wait for anyone else to come and help him. Melody needed to stay in her animal form as long as possible to make the wounds heal more quickly.

He'd made so many mistakes, and there was no way he was ever going to make it all up to her.

10

Melody opened her eyes. She was in her room, tucked snugly into her bed. The miniature Christmas tree she'd set up on the dresser twinkled happily at her, though she didn't remember turning it on. The base of her spine hurt, and her head throbbed. Actually, every part of her hurt. She turned her head to look when the door opened, but that hurt, too.

"Emersyn," she said when she saw her best friend. "I need to talk to you."

"Yes, and there's plenty I need to talk to you about, too." Her face was all business as she set her medical bag on the bench at the foot of the bed and opened it. "But first, I need to see how those wounds are coming along. Bear claws can be a real bitch."

Melody cooperated as Emersyn whisked back the covers and examined the wounds on her sides. She sucked in air through her teeth as Emersyn poked and prodded with her cool fingers. The injury felt hot and swollen.

"There's a small amount of infection, but it's already working its way out of your body," Emersyn said. She pulled a thermometer from her bag and pressed it to Melody's forehead. "You don't have a fever, so I think you're just about in the clear."

"Other than how much it hurts, I guess," Melody groaned as she got back under the sheets. "Those bears were pretty determined."

"Yes, but thanks to you, they're no longer a threat. Also, thanks to you, the children are safe." Emersyn took Melody's hand in her own and looked into her eyes. "I can't tell you what it means to me that you've put your life on the line—twice now—for my son. You're incredible, Melody."

"I didn't do it alone." Melody said it to remind both Emersyn and herself that she'd had help. There'd been Amar, but also Roman. She'd seen him streaking across the yard, his white coat shining in the sun as he came to her aid. She'd felt him, too, inside her head. He'd reached out to her in the same way she'd done to him, but his effort had been far more powerful. Melody wasn't sure whether she should regret the fact that she'd been too busy to reply. "I don't know what I would've done if they hadn't been there. I need to thank them."

"That's going to have to wait a little while. You need your rest. Half the house is heading out to visit Morefield's clan. They're going to assess the situation and see what they need to do next. Gabe and I are staying here, considering that Lucas was involved in the attack. Gabe's with the children right now."

"And the kids are okay? I mean, they have to be somewhat traumatized by the whole thing. I think I might be." Tears pricked her eyes as the memory of that bear charging at her played in slow motion. At the moment, she'd operated purely by instinct and adrenaline. Now, she could slow it all down and examine every aspect of it. That bear would've killed her, and then it would've taken the children. If she'd managed to save them all from the first attacker, the second one surely would've succeeded if it hadn't been for Roman. She could still see them coming at her, their teeth bared. Worst of all, she could still feel the pounding of the earth under her feet as they charged.

Emersyn sat on the edge of the bed. "Ruby is young enough that she probably won't remember any of this, at least not long-term. Lucas won't stop talking about it, in his own way, but it seems he's rather proud of himself for protecting Ruby."

Melody smiled at that thought. "He was really doing his best to be scary."

"So I'm told. I'll leave you to rest, but don't worry. We'll get all this business with Ruby straightened out soon enough." She stood up.

Melody grabbed her hand. "I really do need to talk to you, if you have a minute."

"Of course." Emersyn sat down again. "What is it?"

Swallowing, Melody searched for the right words. Then she reminded herself that she was closer to Emersyn than anyone else in the world. Well, almost anyone. She didn't have to think; she only needed to speak. "I... I lied. I *do* think Roman and I are mates. There's this pull between us that I can't resist. I gave into it a little at first, telling myself that there was nothing wrong with the two of us just having fun. Then it started to feel like it got out of hand, and I got so mad at him. And then he was out there playing with the kids, and I reached out to him with my mind, but I didn't really mean to, and then he stormed off, and maybe that was why..." She broke off from her rambling, crying into the pillow.

"Shh. Honey, don't cry. It's all okay. I know how frustrating and strange it can be when you meet your mate."

"But I don't know what to think about it all," Melody explained, accepting the tissue Emersyn offered her. "One minute we're doing fine, and then the next, it's like he wishes he'd never laid eyes on me."

Emersyn pressed her lips together. "Like any other soldier, I'm sure Roman has some demons from his past that he's trying to deal with. I've noticed the energy between the two of you. I'm sure you'll work it out if you give it time."

Melody shook her head. "That's just the thing, Em. I tried to tell myself that it didn't matter because it would never work with the distance between here and Wyoming. He'd already told me he wasn't going to join the Force. I'm starting to feel, though, like it *does* matter."

Tightening her grip on Melody's hand, Emersyn asked quietly, "What do you want to do about it?"

"Like everything else, I'm still trying to figure it out. But I do know that I can't just give up this chance at actually settling down and being with my mate. I don't know how we would work it all out, whether we'd live here or in Wyoming or somewhere else entirely, but that means there's a chance I wouldn't be able to watch Lucas or run headquarters. Before I even think of talking to Roman about all this, I need to know if you're all right with it. The last thing I want to do is let you down."

"Do you mean because of Lucas?" Emersyn asked. "You must've hit your head when you were fighting off that bear. I love that I have someone here whom I love and trust who watches my son. Lucas means more to me than anything, and even before you proved it in real life, I knew you'd do everything in your power to protect him. Still, he's my son, not yours. You don't have any obligation to stay here, Mel. Gabe and I would figure it out."

Melody nodded and let out a breath. In the back of her mind, she'd known Emersyn would be rational about this. That was always how she was, anyway. "I just didn't want to disappoint you. And what about Roman? Do you think I should go for it?"

Emersyn giggled. "Are you writing his name in little hearts on the inside of a notebook, because I feel like we're in high school! I went through some of that with Gabe, too. Yes, go for it. See how he really feels."

"Yeah." Melody thought about how quickly Roman had shut her down when she'd reached out to him. He'd come right back to her aid a few minutes later, and she could swear he'd been in her mind during the attack, but it still worried her. "What if he rejects me?"

"I doubt he would." Emersyn raised her brows and pinched her mouth, looking sassy. "You're one hell of a catch, Mel. The absolute worst he can do is say no, anyway. Then you'll move on, and you'll get past it. I promise. For right now, though, you rest." She patted Melody's arm, collected her bag, and slipped out of the room.

Melody lay there, staring at the ceiling. Emersyn was right. She couldn't live her life waiting for something to happen and hoping it would all work out. There was nothing wrong with standing up for what she wanted and asking if it could be possible. She wouldn't demand anything from Roman that he wasn't willing to give freely, but Melody had never been such a meek and mild woman to only take the minimum and be all right with it.

Flicking off the covers, she sat up in bed and swung her feet over the side, though the stabbing pain in her ribs made her immediately regret it. That damn bear had done a number on her. She'd heal up soon enough, but she could at least go find Roman.

The door to his room was slightly ajar, and classic rock filtered out through it. Melody smiled, realizing she'd had no idea up until this point what kind of music he liked. There was still so much to learn about him. There was so much more to both of them than just the events over the past few weeks. His visit was going by quickly, but they still had time before he was due back in Wyoming after Christmas. Melody knocked softly.

"Come in," Roman barked.

She pushed the door open to find him standing next to the bed, dressed in jeans and a t-shirt. A suitcase was spread on the comforter, already packed with a neatly folded stack of clothes, a row of socks, and a few books. Roman was in the process of folding another shirt when he looked up at her. He said nothing.

"What's going on?" Alarm bells were clanging in her head, and her heart was pounding so heavily, she could hardly hear the music anymore. "I thought you weren't going back until after Christmas."

"I've changed my mind." He turned away from her as he pulled open a dresser drawer, saw that it was empty, and slammed it shut again. He took a pair of jeans from the next drawer down.

Her throat was thick as she tried to swallow. This

wasn't right. This wasn't what she wanted. She was supposed to have more time. *They* were supposed to have more time. How could they work it all out if he wasn't even in the same state? "Why?"

"There's no reason for me to stay here any longer." He put the jeans in his suitcase and crossed the room to the closet, opening the door wide to double-check that he'd gotten everything.

Roman didn't elaborate, but he didn't need to for Melody to understand. "You could've at least told me."

His eyes met hers for only a fraction of a second. "There's nothing to tell."

"Now, hold on a second." She stepped forward, wincing at the pain in her side once again, but was determined to get past it. "What, exactly, makes you think there isn't anything to tell? At the very least, I'm the one who oversees the daily functions of this house. I think I deserve to know who's coming and going."

"Fine. You do that, Melody. Get your ledger book and note that I'm leaving today, catching a plane, and heading right back to Wyoming where I belong." Roman picked up a pair of shoes from under the bed and slammed them into his suitcase.

Her eyes narrowed. "That's not what I meant."

"Then what did you mean?" he asked, throwing his hands in the air. "What does any of this mean?"

"You're not making sense." She wanted to reach out, grab his arms, and push him down on the bed. She wanted to make him sit and listen to her, to talk this through, to figure it all out in a rational way, but he wasn't going to allow it. Her snow leopard was already reacting, growling in frustration at his stupidity.

"That's fine by me, because there's not a damn bit of my trip here that has made any sense." Roman's brows were a firm line as he zipped up his suitcase. "I came out here because Amar didn't want me to spend the holidays alone. He thought I should be around him and meet all his friends so that he wouldn't have to worry about me. What he didn't realize was that I'm more alone here than I am anywhere else in the fucking world." He breezed past her toward the door.

"Can't we at least just talk about this?" She couldn't let him go without speaking her mind, but right then, she didn't know what to say. How could she tell him she was head-over-heels in love with him and wanted to find a way for them to work out when he was glowering at her from the doorway?

"I wanted to talk to you earlier today, as I recall,

and you refused." Roman shook his head as he set the suitcase down. In two quick strides, he was only inches from her face, and she could feel the heat and tension rising from his body. "Melody, I can't keep doing this. There's something between us, and I don't think either one of us would try to deny that, but every time I turn the corner, there's something else standing in the way of it. Everything I do, everything I feel, and every decision I make is wrong. I'd much rather go be wrong by myself, thank you."

Arguments formed on the tip of her tongue, but they were quickly squashed by the urges of her snow leopard. As angry as she was with him, why did she want to reach out and pull him closer? Why did she want to press her lips against his and fall into bed the way they had that night after watching TV? Why did her big cat constantly remind her that there was so much more going on than what either of them could see on the surface?

No. She couldn't just let her instincts guide her on this. Where would they be if they did nothing but act the way their wild sides demanded them to? Melody wanted to end her spinster streak, but it wasn't worth it if she got stuck with someone who wouldn't even sit and have a rational conversation with her. "Fine. I guess if that's how it is, then who am I to stop you?" She shoved past him and stormed out into the hall, heading back to her room. The doorbell rang, but she ignored it. Someone else could get it.

Tears blurred her eyes, but she blinked them back as she paced cagily in her room. Roman wasn't worth shedding any tears over. He was just another dick, like all the rest of them were. If he'd wanted to be with her, then he would have tried to find a way. It didn't have to be up to her. She shouldn't have to be the one to bow down and say she was wrong when he'd been plenty guilty himself. Melody curled her fists at her sides. Maybe it was time to get out and just take a long run in her feline form. Dashing through the woods and pretending the rest of the world didn't exist sounded like the perfect prescription for what was ailing her.

She bumped into Emersyn again as soon as she left her room. "If you're here to tell me to get my ass back in bed, don't bother. I've been through enough for the time being, and I just need to get outside." Melody put her chin in the air, thoroughly expecting Emersyn or someone else along the way to caution her about the recent attack and how it wasn't safe.

But Emersyn shook her head. "You probably should be in bed, but I actually came to give you some news. Kent just called. They were able to deal with the Alpha and beta of the clan who kidnapped Ruby. Apparently, it was a scheme hatched by the two of them. They were planning on returning her in exchange for territorial rights, but her capture wasn't something the rest of the clan agreed upon. They're dealing with all of that, but the important thing is that Ruby's parents are on their way here to pick her up."

The world swirled in Melody's vision, and the edges darkened until she could see only Emersyn's face. "Are you serious?" she whispered.

A steady arm wrapped around her. "Yes. Ruby's parents had been working hard to get their baby back, but they didn't know what had happened to her or that she was here. They thought she was still in the custody of Morefield's clan, so they and their clanmates launched several attacks against the Morefields. That was how it all came to light to the rest of the bears. Mr. Morefield and his beta are being forced to step down. Ironically, it was Morefield's wife who'd told Amar and Roman about the kidnapping and had arranged for her to be dropped off here, and she's now the one who will become the new Alpha."

Clan politics might have been interesting to

Melody at any other time, but not right now. The only thing she understood was that two of the people she'd come to take so much joy in were being taken away from her. There was still the rest of the Force, and her work for them, and especially little Lucas, but she still felt as though her heart was being ripped straight out of her chest. "I know it's not fair of me to say this," she sobbed into Emersyn's arms, "but I don't want Ruby to go."

"I know, honey. I know. She's meant the world to you. And you're the kindest, sweetest, most wonderful person because I know you would've taken care of Ruby for the rest of her life if that was what was needed. But her parents need her right now."

"They must be so relieved to know she's safe," Melody replied, trying to console herself. Everything hurt so badly, but her injuries were the least of it. "How long until they get here?"

"Kent didn't say, but I'm sure they're coming as quickly as they can."

Melody nodded. "I want to say goodbye to her."

"Of course. She's right down the hall in the nursery." Emersyn guided the way, and even though Melody knew it well, she still leaned on her friend for support. "Gabe, I think we need to give Melody and Ruby a minute."

Gabe looked up from where he'd been playing on the floor with the two children. He didn't question his mate as he scooped up Lucas and headed into the hall. "Let's go see if we can find a snack, buddy."

"Snack? Ruby?"

"That's okay, Ruby will get a snack later."

Emersyn touched Melody's back. "I'll give you two some time, but I won't be far. Just call if you need me." She closed the door gently behind her.

Melody grabbed a tissue from the dresser and blotted her eyes. "You poor thing. You don't want to see me this way, but I can't help it. I've just fallen in love with you so much over the last couple of weeks." She fell to her knees in front of Ruby's bouncy seat.

Ruby responded with a playful kick of her feet and a grin.

"Oh, I know. You're so young, and you don't understand the tragedy of all this. I'm so grateful for that. I'm so glad that you probably won't remember this at all, because I know it would be so hard for an older child to go through. But I'm also so terribly sad that you won't remember it, because I want you to remember me." Melody cried harder as she unbuckled the straps and lifted Ruby into her arms. "You've been a very precious little thing to me, Ruby. I hope that you'll understand that."

A gentle knock came on the door, and it opened a second later. "Melody, honey. Her parents are here."

"Okay. Let's go, sweet one. Time to go see Mommy and Daddy."

Emersyn held out her arms. "Would you rather I take her?"

"No. I need to do this myself." She knew it was true. She was heartbroken enough over Roman, and there was little she could do about it. But she could do herself the favor of being the one to hand Ruby over, to see her parents, to know she was doing the right thing. It would be a type of closure for her, even if it hurt.

Emersyn nodded. "I'll gather her things."

Downstairs, a couple was standing near the front door. Jude and Reid stood nearby, and that let Melody know that these people really were who they said they were. She knew the two brothers, who'd been orphaned as children, would never let Ruby be handed into the wrong arms. That thought made Melody realize how much comfort she'd taken in the little things that the Force offered. It wasn't just the fact that she had a roof over her head, a steady job, and a sense of satisfaction that came from getting things done. It was that she knew these people and all their little idiosyncrasies. She knew what to expect from them, and she knew she could count on them.

Jude made the introductions. "Melody, this is Allison and Matthew Wilson. Ruby's parents."

"Hi," Melody said with a forced smile as she blinked back her tears. "My name is Melody. I've been taking care of Ruby for these past few weeks."

"Oh!" Allison swooped in to take her daughter. "Oh, my sweet baby! My little princess! I've missed you so much! I've been so worried about you!"

Ruby replied with an enthusiastic coo, her arms and legs bunching in and punching out in excitement as she saw her mother again.

There were tears in Matthew's eyes as he stroked his baby girl's back and turned to Melody. "Jude and Reid told us what good care you've been taking of her. I admit we were relieved when we found out she was with the SOS Force, but it makes me feel even better to see how happy and healthy she is. We can't thank you enough." His wife was bawling too hard to even respond.

Melody understood that sentiment, as she could no longer stop herself from crying. "It was my pleasure. I know you already know, but your daughter is such a sweet, amazing little thing. And she's so cute when she shifts into her bear cub." She laughed through her tears at the memory of Ruby chasing after Lucas in the yard.

Matthew and Allison looked at each other in shock. "She shifted in front of you?"

"She sure did." Alarm bells went off in Melody's mind. She would feel terrible if that'd been the first time their daughter had taken on her animal form and they weren't around to see it. "Hasn't she done it before? She didn't seem to have any trouble with it."

"She has," Matthew replied, his thumb gliding over the back of Ruby's head in awe, as though he was seeing her for the first time. "It's just that we've found she only does it in front of those she's extremely comfortable around, such as ourselves and our parents. Even the rest of our clan hasn't seen her change before. You really are something special, Melody."

"Yes, she is," Emersyn replied for her, putting her arm around her friend once again. "We're just so glad we found you. I've gathered up Ruby's things, including her blanket. We had ordered some clothes for her, as well, so she'll have some new outfits."

"What can we do to repay you?" Allison asked.

"Not a thing," Melody said. "Having time with Ruby was enough." She turned, not waiting to see Ruby leave, not wanting to press her forehead to the window as she watched her parents load her into their vehicle and drive off to live her life. Melody would get past this at some point, she knew. She had to, and they said that time healed all wounds. But it sure as hell hurt right now.

11

"You're sure this is what you want to do?" Amar asked as they sped toward the airport.

Roman was starting to regret letting Amar drive him there. It would've been easier to just get up early, sneak off before anyone else had gotten out of bed, and waste time in the lounge, but he'd felt he owed it to his old friend to do a little more than that. "Yes. I'm sure."

"But it's not even officially Christmas yet," Amar countered.

"That's true," Roman said with a nod. "And that's exactly why it's a good idea to fly right now. I can get back to Wyoming in time to wish all my cattle and horses a very Merry Christmas."

"Even with all the traffic that's bound to be at the

airport? Come on, Roman. I know you don't like crowds, and we both remember how difficult it was to get stateside too close to a holiday when we were on leave." He checked his mirrors and changed lanes. "It'd be much easier if you just stayed at headquarters and had Christmas with us. Hell, stay until New Year's. We can ring it in together. It's a lot more fun doing it in a warm and comfortable home instead of in a mess hall on the other side of the world."

Roman couldn't argue with that. "I'm sure you're right. I'm sure that it'll also be nice to ring in the new year at home in Sheridan, maybe with a few of my new clanmates, lifting up beers and belching into the night in a remote cabin where we don't have to worry about women."

Amar nodded. "Uh huh."

"What?" Roman's muscles tensed. He hadn't really thought he'd get anything past his friend and comrade. Amar saw and noted everything. That didn't mean Roman wanted to talk about it.

"It's a woman thing," Amar replied.

"Isn't everything a woman thing?" Roman challenged.

Amar laughed. "Sure, I guess that's true. You could make the argument that you fought for your country, putting your life on the line because you wanted to keep the women safe. You could stretch that out and make further arguments about major life decisions being based on women somehow. That doesn't mean you made the right ones."

"You don't have to be the wise old dragon all the time, you know. You could just let me do what I want and call it good enough." Roman looked out the window, squinting against the bright sunshine and all those damn palm trees. It didn't look like Christmas or even winter around there, and he was getting tired of it.

"I could, but I wouldn't be much of a friend if I didn't call you out on your mistakes."

Roman sighed. "I already explained all this. Being a dad just isn't in the cards for me, and Melody is far better off without me. I would only get in the way of her dreams. Even if—and that's a big *if* —the two of us could work it out for a little while, it would just end up falling apart, leaving the two of us even more miserable."

Amar was silent for a long time as they floated along the expressway. Roman glanced at him a couple of times, surprised that he wasn't making any further arguments or trying to rope him into joining the Force again.

"Thanks for helping us with the Morefield clan," he finally said. "The rest of the crew and I work well together, but it's always nice to get a fresh perspective on things."

"No problem. Do you think Mrs. Morefield will do all right as the Alpha?" Roman figured it would all work out well enough, and it wasn't really any of his business, but it was easier to make conversation about matters that didn't directly involve him.

"I don't have the least bit of doubt. I admit I was a little shocked to find out the woman in the flower bed was the Alpha's wife, but after talking to her more recently, I know she'll do well. The rest of the clan, it turns out, didn't like her husband very much, but they do think quite a lot of her. She has the backing of the rest of her clan as well as the Force, so there won't be any further problems from them."

"Good. And I heard that Ruby's parents came to get her, so everything is back to normal." Roman turned to look out the window again. There had been a little chaos while he was in California, but it had all settled now. Roman would leave before any further trouble started.

Amar ran his hand across his face, scratching his fingers through the dark stubble that had recently grown in. "Did you happen to talk to Melody before we left?"

So much for keeping the conversation on other subjects. "No. I doubt she'd want to hear anything I have to say."

"Yeah, maybe you're right."

Roman snapped his head around to look at his friend.

"Well, she was really upset about Ruby going home as it was. The last thing she needs is for you to complicate things when you're just leaving anyway." He slid the car over into the drop-off lane in front of the airport. "You let me know when you want to come down for another visit. I'll be happy to have you. I might even pick your sorry ass up at the gate if you ask me nicely." He flashed a grin from the driver's seat.

"I don't know if I had the chance to tell you this, Amar, but you haven't changed a bit." Roman shook his head and laughed as he retrieved his bags from the trunk and headed into the terminal.

He made his way through check-in and security. The airport was horribly crowded. Parents yelled at each other as they tried to keep track of their children, people swayed restlessly as they queued up for overpriced coffee, and young businessmen in suits carried out their deals loudly on their phones. Roman just wanted to get past all of it and back to the peace and quiet of Wyoming, and he was grateful for the short wait at the gate.

Though he hadn't meant to, he ended up next to the window to accommodate a young couple who wanted to sit together. They whispered excitedly to each other, her hand touching his arm, his hand touching her leg. The seats were too close together for Roman to scoot his hulking frame any further away from them, but they were oblivious anyway. He spent the rest of his flight concentrating on all the ranch work that awaited him when he got back home, purposely keeping Melody from his mind.

The plane landed with a thump that woke him up. Roman had been dreaming, but seeing the runway stream by through the window made him forget what it had been about. He was there. He was back home in Wyoming, right where he belonged. His new clan was there, and they wouldn't create the sort of drama he'd been living through over the last few weeks. It would all just be work as usual, and that was exactly what he needed.

As eager as he was to get off the plane, and even though he knew exactly where his one carry-on was stowed, his best-laid plans to get off a plane quickly never worked out. There were always too many people in the aisle, blocking the way as they stumbled over feet and purses to find their bags and get themselves together. Roman had often found this annoying. It wasn't as though it was a surprise that the plane had landed when it did; they ought to have been prepared for it. Moreover, they ought to have had a little more courtesy and organization so they could've disembarked in an orderly fashion. People, however, were much like cattle. The most you could hope for was that they'd be walking in the right direction.

Stepping into the airport, Roman was greeted with a blast of hot air and the sound of Christmas music ringing in his ears. Someone had decorated the place with cheap plastic garland and a sad old Christmas tree that should've been put out of its misery long ago. Faded gold ornaments dangled from its sagging branches.

Roman didn't want to see any of that as it was. He wasn't in the holiday spirit, but it was all the more aggravating because it made him think of Melody. If she had been there, she would've had the whole place glitzed up to the nines, with a beautiful tree, tons of lights, and little touches that would make all the difference. He thought of that sprig of holly that had been in her hair that first night he'd met her. He could easily imagine himself reaching up and taking it out, watching as her hair tumbled down in a cloud of untamed fire.

No. The whole reason he'd come back early was to get away from Melody, and that meant physically as well as emotionally. He had no place in her life, and she had no place in his. This was how it was supposed to be. Who cared that their inner animals had created such chaos? He could restore balance by force, and he would do just that.

Roman trudged through the airport, his carry-on bag slung over his shoulder. The Sheridan County Airport was much smaller than the one he'd left just a few hours ago, and he was grateful for it. He'd get his suitcase and be on his way.

"There he is!" someone called off to his left.

"Hold up your sign, so he'll see it! Nice and tall, just like that. Great job!"

"Daddy!"

Roman turned, as did everyone else in the terminal, to see a family standing in a cluster, holding up a big sign that said, "Welcome Home, Daddy!" on it. The family was all dressed in their Christmas pajamas and furry boots, and someone even had a huge velvet sack full of presents dragging along on the ground.

A man who'd just come from the gate locked eyes with the family. He dropped his bags and ran straight for them, scooping the little boy holding the sign up into his arms, swinging him around in a big circle.

Roman looked away. This wasn't any of his business. People had reunions in airports all the time. It only made sense. And he couldn't even feel sorry for himself about no one picking him up since he hadn't bothered to let any of his clan know he was coming home early. Old Henry would be thrilled when Roman showed up at home to take over all the work and care that went into running the place, though.

"Baby!"

Unable to help himself, Roman turned back toward the family. The mother had broken off from her children, her eyes soft and wet as she stepped toward her husband. She touched his cheeks, taking a long moment just to look at him before she wrapped her arms around his neck. He murmured something in her ear that couldn't be heard at this distance, but Roman could guess it was all about how much they loved each other and how much they'd hated being apart for so long.

Roman tightened his grip on his bag as he continued toward baggage claim, joining the line of passengers who stood patiently while they waited for a familiar piece of luggage to come circling around on the conveyor belt. It was nice that the family he'd seen could have a relationship like that. He had no doubt they'd probably all sit down right there in the terminal to exchange presents and take a bunch of pictures that their friends and family would all pretend to be enthusiastic about.

But romantic notions like that weren't real. They were just ridiculous fantasies that people created because they sounded nice, and they believed them for as long as they could. They were just something that would dissipate over time and leave everyone disappointed.

And they were exactly what he wanted to experience with Melody.

Though it was easy to believe that romance was just fiction for everyone else and even for himself, he couldn't actually believe that about her. She'd proven it in the way she'd decorated headquarters, not because she was asked to, but because she liked it. Then there was her love for old Christmas movies, and how she didn't seem to care that the two of them were eating leftovers in their pajamas in the middle of the night, as long as they were spending time together. She'd sprung into action when she'd heard Ruby crying on the doorstep, even though at that time, she had no idea whose child it was and had no obligation to take care of it.

Roman stepped forward to grab his suitcase as he remembered the way she'd looked just before he'd left. He hadn't stopped to talk to her, knowing he was only going to make things worse, but he'd caught a glimpse of her face, swollen from all the tears she'd cried. He wanted to blame all of those tears on her separation from Ruby, but deep down, he knew it wasn't just that. He'd caused plenty of them, and she deserved better.

That last part was what had convinced him that he'd been right to change his flight and leave early. Roman loved her, and he'd known that early on, but he'd also known he wasn't right for her. He was too stubborn, too overbearing, and too damn selfish. He was also too dumb to realize what an amazing opportunity he'd passed up, and he'd made an awful mistake.

12

"You okay, Mel'dy? You okay?" Lucas bent down in front of Melody, his hands on his knees, and peered into her face.

"I'm just tired, buddy. You're very kind for asking, though." She smiled at him, glad to know that he truly did care about her. Someone else might think of it as a small comfort, but there was nothing better than concern from a sweet, innocent child.

"Nap?" Lucas asked, pointing upstairs.

Melody pulled him into her arms. He'd lost that baby scent that she enjoyed so much, and instead, he smelled like Goldfish crackers and Play-Doh, but she loved it anyway. "No, I don't want to take a nap right now. Maybe later."

"Mel'dy nap." Lucas headed for the couch, where

he pulled down a throw pillow. He put it on the floor and put his hands on her head, slowly guiding her down toward it.

Who was she to interfere when he was trying so hard to take care of her? "That's very nice. Thank you, Lucas."

But he wasn't done. He next pulled down a soft blanket that they kept draped over the back of the couch. It took him a lot of effort to cover her, and her backside was still hanging out by the time he was done, but he looked pleased with himself. "There. Mel'dy nap."

"A very nice nap, indeed," Melody replied. "You want to lay down here with me?"

"Okay." He stretched out on the rug next to her.

Melody covered him with some of the blanket. She reached for the remote and turned on the TV, grateful for a little bit of downtime. Her separation from Roman had been much harder on her than she'd thought possible, and so had Ruby's absence. She'd considered asking Jude for the Wilsons' phone number so she could offer to babysit, but she was worried about coming off like a weirdo.

As Christmas cartoons jangled brightly on the television in front of her, she allowed herself a fantasy of what things might've been like if the world had been a different place. What if she and Roman could have actually worked things out? What if they'd never fought in the first place? Melody hardly cared whether they lived in Wyoming, California, or Timbuktu, and she imagined them living out their fictional relationship in some nondescript home that could have been anywhere. Maybe they would even have had a child or two. Roman would have gotten the hang of the kid thing. In fact, he already had a better handle on it than he realized, Melody was sure.

"Melody?"

She opened her eyes. The cartoon on the screen had changed completely. Lucas was still curled up with her, fortunately, or she'd have felt even more terrible as she looked up at Emersyn standing over her. "Hey. I guess I fell asleep. Lucas had me very well tucked in."

"I can see that."

Melody sat up, and Lucas scooted closer to the television. "I told him I was tired, and he insisted. It was really cute." She pressed her hand to her forehead, feeling drained even after her little snooze.

"You doing okay? I know the last few days haven't been easy on you." Emersyn sat on the edge of the couch and folded her hands between her knees.

"They haven't, but I'm fine. I just need to catch up on a little sleep, and I'd better do it soon. I'd planned to have all my shopping done early, but that got put on hold by...you know, so I still have a few things to pick up. And then I've still got to get everything wrapped. I have a big grocery trip to make, too." She pushed back the blanket and stood up. Black waves spiraled in toward the center of her vision, and she stumbled backward.

"Whoa. Are you sure you're all right?" Emersyn reached out to grab her hand and led her toward the sofa.

"It's just a little holiday stress, that's all." Melody looked up at her best friend, and when she saw the compassion in her eyes, it made her want to cry. She'd thought she'd run out of tears a long time ago, yet there they were, threatening to spill over once again. "I think."

"You think? Tell me everything that's happening. Don't skip a bit of it." Emersyn was back in doctor mode.

Melody knew that was not a force to be reckoned with. "I'm having trouble sleeping. I spend half the day feeling like I want to throw up and the other half feeling like I'm going to cry. I'm just stressed out."

Emersyn patted her hand and stood up. "Why don't you step into my office for a minute?"

"But Lucas—"

"He's entertained, and we'll be right in the next room. Alessia's in the kitchen, so she can keep an eye on him, too. Come on." Emersyn brought her through a doorway and into the exam room. She reached into a cabinet and fetched a small cup with a lid. "Let's start with a pregnancy test."

The blood drained from Melody's face. Somehow, even as rational of a person as she normally was, she hadn't even thought about that. "I don't think that's necessary."

Emersyn's face was challenging. "Is there even the slightest chance?"

"Well, I mean, yeah..."

The doctor forced the plastic cup into Melody's hand. "Then pee."

A couple of minutes later, Melody shifted her weight from one foot to the other as she awaited the results. "I hadn't really thought about this, you know. I mean, I always wanted children, but what if—"

"Save the what-ifs for just a minute longer," Emersyn advised, "until you know for sure. I know how much you like to plan things out, but in this case, whatever will be will be."

"Yeah. I guess so." It was impossible not to think about it, though. Melody had found one of Ruby's little pink rompers mixed in with the laundry. Her parents had shown up unexpectedly, and the item had been missed. Melody had taken it back to her room and tucked it away in a drawer, unsure of what to do with it. She couldn't possibly go visit them with the outfit as an excuse; it would hurt too much.

"Mel?"

"Yeah?"

Emersyn turned the test around so she could see. "You're going to be a mother. Congratulations."

Melody clapped her hands to her mouth. "Oh, my God. Are you sure?"

"Are you questioning my medical degree?" Emersyn retorted, laughing. "Of course, I'm sure. This is so exciting! You're going to have a little one!"

"Wow," Melody breathed. Just a second ago, she'd been making plans for the next eighteen years of her life, but in that moment, she just wanted to quiet her brain and take it all in. This was it. It hadn't happened the way she'd imagined, but it was most certainly happening.

"That's one heck of a Christmas present," Emersyn said with a smile as she put everything away and stripped off her gloves. "I'm so happy for you, Melody."

"Thanks. I—I don't even know what to think or do or say." Melody wandered out to the living room, where Lucas was still happily watching TV. She looked down at him and his adorable face. That would be her life from now on. She wouldn't just be watching someone else's child, but her own. There would be late nights and long days and tons of diapers and more laundry than she could ever keep up with. There would be times when she'd be so frustrated, she wouldn't know what to do next, but the one thing she was sure of was that she'd be the happiest woman in the world.

"If you don't like the color, just let me know and I'll make you a different one," Melody said.

"Are you kidding me?" Emersyn ran her hands up and down the length of the bright red scarf she'd just pulled out of the gift bag. "It's so pretty and so soft!"

"I just have to wonder when you had time to make it," Gabe added, reaching over to touch it. "You're too busy for something like that."

Melody waved off the compliments. She was already feeling a glow unlike anything she'd experienced in her life. As much as she loved Christmas and seeing her friends get their gifts, she knew it wasn't from that. It was from the miracle that was growing inside her, the one that would change the rest of her life. "Hey, I've been planning this holiday for months. And don't be too flattered. You're just my guinea pigs for learning how to knit."

"I think you did just fine," Alessia marveled as she also pulled out a scarf, hers in a pale green that matched her eyes. "I'll be wearing this all the time!"

Lucas was just as enthusiastic as the others as he took out the thick blanket she'd made for him. He immediately rolled himself up in it and pretended to take a nap on the floor, much to the delight of all the adults watching.

The morning went far too quickly, with everyone up early and ready to get started. The ring of presents around the tree that had extended halfway across the living room was soon reduced to shredded paper and boxes, all headed for recycling, as everyone gathered their prizes and took them off to their respective rooms or packed them into their vehicles to head home.

Melody lingered, touching a little glass ornament on the tree and wishing it didn't have to be over with so soon. There was a thrill to seeing all the decorations up at the end of November, but by the time Christmas came and went, most of it lost its magic.

Amar stepped into the room. "Melody, I'm glad you're here. I wanted to tell you how wonderful everything looked."

"You already told me that when I put it all up a month ago," she said with a smile as she adjusted one of the tree's baubles. "I'll give it another day or two, but then I'll get it all put up in the attic."

His dark eyes grew serious at the suggestion. "Don't you dare! There are plenty of hands here to help you, and I don't want you to hurt yourself."

"Okay, okay. You do have a point on the heavy lifting. But," she leveled her gaze at him and tried her best to look authoritative, "I'll personally be in charge of getting all the delicates wrapped and put away. I don't trust any of you brutes to do it correctly."

He put his hands in the air. "Wouldn't dream of it!" Amar hesitated, glancing over his shoulder. Melody didn't think he meant to, but she caught his eyes flick to her stomach and then away again. He rubbed the back of his neck with one hand. "I also just wanted you to know…I mean…anything you might need, we're here for you. All of us."

"Thank you. I know, and I appreciate it."

"And I'm sorry."

She'd just been turning back to the tree, but she flicked her head back around to look at him. "What do you mean?"

Amar shrugged. "I was the one who asked Roman to come here in the first place. We've always been good friends, and even though I knew he wasn't perfect, I genuinely didn't think there would be any problems. I just feel like there was something more I could've done, and I don't want you to be in a bad situation because of it."

Melody rested her hand on his arm. Amar was a formidable Alpha, a true dragon at heart who didn't get sappy about anything. It tickled her to see him show a little bit of his softer side, but she knew he was being very sincere about this. She owed it to him to return the favor. "Amar, don't be sorry, and don't feel like any of this is your fault. It hurts to think of Roman, and I can't help but think about him constantly, knowing that I'm carrying his child. It's just something I'm going to have to work through, and I know I will."

"Have you told him yet?"

Melody shook her head. "No. I wanted to give myself a little time to get used to it, to be able to find all the right words. I'll do it soon, though. After Christmas."

"Okay," Amar said with a nod. "I know it's not really my business, but he'd be devastated if he didn't know."

Melody wasn't so sure about that. She was willing to gamble that Roman would be scared or maybe even angry when he found out. The one thing she had to make sure of was that, no matter how she felt or how he acted, she wouldn't try to pull any sort of commitment out of him. "Don't worry. I'll do it."

"Thanks. Katalin and I are planning to have dinner out later on tonight if you'd like to join us."

"That's all right." Melody knew how much the two of them were in love. She didn't want to spoil their holiday together, nor was she sure she could stomach all that romance right in front of her. "I've got some other things I'm going to take care of."

Amar looked doubtful, but he turned and headed out of the room.

Melody ran her fingers over the strand of garland on the mantel and straightened the stockings hung in front of the fireplace. Most of them were just for show, but Gabe and Emersyn had weighted Lucas's down with snacks, fruit, and little toys. He would be eating out of that overgrown sock for a couple of weeks, at least.

On an impulse, Melody returned to the tree. She took down a miniature stocking ornament and brought it back over to the mantel, hanging it on top of hers. It was so tiny that it looked silly compared to the rest, but she knew what it meant.

A heavy, urgent knock sounded at the front door. Melody's instincts turned on high, her snow leopard at the ready as she crossed the room, wondering what kind of drama would be on the other side of the door this time.

Roman stood there on the doorstep. For the longest moment, his bags in his hands, he simply stared at her. "Melody."

"Roman." She glanced over her shoulder, wondering if anyone else had known he was coming. "What are you doing here? I thought you went back to Wyoming." Melody held the door open wider for him to come in.

"I did, and I felt like an absolute piece of shit for it." Roman stepped inside and tossed his bags down in the entryway. "I need to talk to you."

"All right." If he'd asked her that a few days ago,

she would've told him to just shove it. But Melody needed to talk to him, too. "We can go in the living room. We just finished up Christmas and everyone is pretty much gone." Why was she babbling like that?

He stopped in front of the Christmas tree and took her hand. "I owe you an apology and an explanation."

"No, you don't—"

"Yes." His eyes were serious as they bored into hers, and he was holding both of her hands in his now. "Yes, I do. You see, I thought I found the person I wanted to be with while I was still in the military. We tried to make it work, even while I was overseas. Elizabeth told me she was pregnant with my child, and I couldn't have been more excited. Whatever problems the two of us had, I knew we could work them out because we were going to have a baby together. I fell in love with that little boy through video calls and letters and photographs, but when I got home, I found out he wasn't really mine after all."

"Oh, Roman." Melody was too emotional for this, and the corners of her eyes stung with threatening tears. "I'm so sorry."

He shook his head. "I was devastated, too hurt to consider fatherhood again. When I started feeling things with you—not just things, but big things—I knew we were experiencing something real. But if I wasn't emotionally ready to be a father, and if you were destined to be a mother, as I know you are, then I just didn't see a way to work it out."

She touched his cheek as she looked over every aspect of his handsome face.

Roman sighed, looking down for a moment. "I think, in some ways, I know how you must've felt when Ruby's parents came to take her away from you. You had the time to get attached, and you knew there was a chance it would be forever. It wasn't fair of me to just leave you to grieve like that."

"I'm dealing with it," she replied, a small smile playing on the corners of her lips.

"It also wasn't fair of me to flip out on you after the incident at the zoo. I never meant to make you feel like you were incompetent. It just scared the hell out of me to think something could've happened to you. Then when it happened again in the backyard, I just felt that fear all over again. I had to leave, and maybe I still should, but I had to come back here and tell you."

Melody squeezed his fingers. "You didn't have to come all the way back to California just to explain your past to me."

"Maybe not, but I did need to come back to give you these." Roman reached into his pocket. He pulled out a closed fist and held it over her hand, releasing a little pile of burgundy rose petals into her palm.

"Zuzu's petals," she said with tears in her eyes. This was the best apology she'd ever gotten, though she thought she might cry all over the velvety little things. "It's Zuzu's petals. You remembered."

"Of course, I did. I can't forget a single moment when I'm with you, Melody. I know we're meant to be together, and I promise I'll stop acting like an ass if you can just give me a chance to love you the way I should." He held her wrist so delicately in his big hand, the petals vibrating between them.

"Roman." Melody fell into his arms and kissed him, her tears streaming back as her snow leopard purred its content. This was what she needed. *Roman* was what she needed. They'd had their little squabble, but that was all over now and everything was going to be different. She pulled back as she realized just how different everything really was going to be.

"What's wrong?" His shoulders sagged as she left his embrace.

Melody kept her arms resting on his, not wanting to let go but knowing she had to do this.

"First, I need to apologize to you, too. You tried to talk to me about all this, and I was too stubborn to let you. I didn't make things any better, and I guess I thought it would be easier."

"It's all right, Melody."

"But there's more." She pulled in a deep breath. There hadn't been enough time to find the right words. Instead, she reached out to the fireplace and picked up the mini stocking she'd hung there next to her own. "If we're going to be together, you need to know that it won't just be the two of us."

He took a step back, but he tightened his grip on her arm as he automatically looked down at her stomach. "Are you sure?"

"Very. Emersyn confirmed it herself."

Roman took the tiny stocking from her hand. Tears glistened in his eyes as he ran his thumb over the glittery rickrack at the top of it. "Melody, this is the best Christmas present I ever could've gotten."

They fell against each other once again. Melody roved her tongue over his, tasting him as a thrill of Christmas magic ran up and down her spine. Her body was alive as she pressed herself against him, and her snow leopard leaped inside her. This was where she was meant to be. It didn't matter what state or even what side of the world they were in, as long as they were together.

Roman scooped his hands underneath her, easily swinging her into the air and carrying her up the staircase, pausing on the landing to kiss her again. "You're so beautiful."

"Are you still going to say that when I'm as big as a house?" she challenged.

He laughed as he went up the second flight of stairs and down the hall. "You'll be the prettiest house I've ever seen."

Melody thumped the side of her fist into his broad chest, liking the way his hard muscles bounced beneath her hand. "Beast."

"You don't even know." Roman shouldered open her bedroom door. He held her high over the bed, making it look as though he would simply drop her in place, but he lowered her gently to the covers and kissed her forehead as he kicked the door shut behind them. He pushed her back down as she started to sit up. "No, you need to relax."

"I'm plenty relaxed," she argued with a smile.

"Not the way I want you to be." He took off her shoes and placed them on the floor next to the bed. Next came her socks, her pants, and her festive sweater. His lips pressed hotly against her cooling skin as he traced a curving line along the top of her breasts, dipping down between them as he unclasped the front closure of her bra. He moved down along the lines of her stomach, kissing her navel as he slowly slipped off her panties. His hands moved back up her legs, squeezing tightly and releasing the tension in her muscles.

Melody moaned softly, not having realized until then just how knotted up she'd been. "Oh, that feels good."

"And I'm just getting started." Roman worked his way up and down her legs. He rubbed down her arms and even swept his hands over her breasts before asking her to roll over.

Melody complied instantly, unable to get enough of this. "You're going to spoil me," she said, her voice halting in the middle of it as he straddled her from behind and worked the knots out of her neck.

"That's the point, isn't it?" His fingers dug pleasantly into her flesh and up onto her scalp.

Goosebumps erupted all over her skin. "That means I'll have to find a way to spoil you, too."

His breath was warm against the back of her neck. "Don't worry. I'm sure you'll figure it out." Those magic hands roved down her backside and to her legs once again, and he dropped kisses all the way.

"There's something distinctly unfair about this situation," Melody remarked as he finally let go of her. She rolled over and sat on the edge of the bed, taking a moment just to put her hands around him and lean against him. He felt so solid and strong. She was always trying to be strong herself, but it was nice to know she wouldn't have to be the only one. His skin was warm and inviting, radiating heat through his clothes. "I think I just want to get you naked to cuddle in bed with me all day," she said as she slowly began unbuttoning his shirt.

"I'm up for that, but I can't promise you I'll behave myself. Not with such a gorgeous woman at my side." He ran his fingers through her hair as she pushed his shirt back from his hard abs and ran her hands over his chest. His dark hair narrowed into a promising trail at the waistband of his jeans, and she unbuckled his belt to see just where it led. Melody skimmed her palms over his backside as she removed his pants and his boxer briefs.

Naked, the two of them moved backward onto the bed together, their skin sliding pleasurably against each other as they got between the sheets, and Melody felt her spirit lift to new heights she'd never experienced before. Roman held her close as he made love to her, worshipping every part of her body with his hands and his mouth, murmuring how much he loved her in her ear. The best part was that she actually believed him. She'd spent far too much of her life thinking she would never truly be loved by someone, that the fairytale endings were for everyone but her, yet it was happening right before her eyes. Her body ripened in his hands as he pulled her close, his hardness insistent against her inner thigh.

"I love you, Melody," he said with one more kiss, his rough palms on either side of her face as he looked into her eyes. "I've loved you from the minute I saw you, and I don't ever want to let you out of my sight again."

"I love you, too, Roman. So much."

He plunged into her then, and as full of passion she already was, Melody discovered there was even more. She surged and rolled with him, her hips moving of their own volition to keep time with his, her hands continually finding some new, exciting plane of his hard body to explore. The morning light streamed through the window, illuminating their bodies and making a gleaming halo around his hair as he pleasured her. Roman moved so carefully, yet she felt the intensity and desperation in his shaking muscles as he sought to claim as much of her as he could.

Melody closed her eyes, letting the rest of the world melt away as she gave herself over completely to this feeling. She focused on the way his body felt inside hers, throbbing in perfect harmony with her heart, and how both her human and snow leopard sides reveled in the soul connection between them. Her breath caught in her throat as her muscles wound up like a spring, clenching tighter and tighter until she could hardly even breathe.

Roman must have felt it, too, because she felt his girth expand, filling her even more. That was enough to push her over the edge, making that knot of muscle melt in an instant as she let go. She clenched her jaw and clawed at his back as their flesh spoke to each other in an ancient exchange they couldn't control.

Her mind buzzing and her muscles quivering, Melody curled up in the crook of his arm as Roman pulled the covers over the two of them. She listened to his heartbeat, knowing that soon enough, they'd both be listening to another heartbeat that was developing in her belly. This had been the perfect Christmas.

13

"Roman! Have you finally returned to us?" Austin strode forward through the terminal and embraced his clanmate. Roman recognized him immediately, with his lantern jaw, piercing eyes, and signature Stetson. "And I take it this is the lovely Melody. I hope that little charter plane wasn't too interesting of a ride." He swept off his hat and kissed her hand.

"It's nice to meet you," she said, blushing a little.

"Old Henry said to tell you everything's fine at the ranch," Austin said as he took Melody's bags from her.

"I hope he didn't have too much trouble taking care of my part of things," Roman hedged. He'd hated to ask anyone to do that much work for him, but he couldn't exactly just leave all the livestock to fend for themselves.

Austin shook his head. "I don't think he minded at all, really. He doesn't have an excuse to get out into the fresh air as much as he'd like to these days. In fact, it also gave him an excuse to head over to my place every night and give me a full report on what he'd done."

The older bear was a beloved member of the clan, and Roman had come to like him just as much as everyone else did. "I'll owe him big for this."

Austin paused at the doors out to the parking lot. "You'd better zip up your coat, Melody. It's a lot colder here than where you came from."

"Oh, look at all this snow!" she squealed as they headed for Austin's truck. "I just love it."

Roman took her hand. He'd missed it too, and it was all the better now that he had her there with him. He chuckled at her enthusiasm. "You haven't seen much of anything yet. We haven't even left the airport parking lot."

"I don't care! I saw plenty through the plane window, but I don't think I'll ever get over all this snow. Everyone's just carrying on about their business as if nothing's happened." She slipped a little, leaning on Roman for support.

"It's just a way of life up here," Roman explained. "They're prepared for it, too. They always have the plows out on the main roads, and everyone has four-wheel-drive vehicles. This will be my first full winter here, but even I know to keep plenty of provisions on hand, just in case. It's nothing like L.A." He hoisted the bags into the back of Austin's truck and held the door open for Melody.

The two of them slipped into the back to sit next to each other. "That's exactly what I'm going to love about it," Melody replied as she buckled in. "There are a lot of great things about L.A., but I was ready for a change of scenery. Can you imagine how wonderful Christmas is going to be up here?"

Austin glanced at her in the rearview. "You like Christmas, huh? Well, then I'll give you the grand tour." He turned the truck toward Main Street, slowing down so Melody could take in all the garland, wreaths, and lights that decorated the downtown area.

"This is amazing!" Melody squealed.

Roman put his hand affectionately on her thigh. When the two of them had sat down and talked about where they'd live, he hadn't been sure that Wyoming was the right choice. Roman had known that was what he'd wanted. Though he'd originally chosen it because of his urge to be alone, he'd come to love it and the grizzly clan that had adopted him. He'd worried that Melody would choose to go back there with him not because she genuinely wanted to, but because she felt she had to. They'd talked well into the night, weighing all the pros and cons of all the decisions that rested on their shoulders. The fact that they could discuss it like mature adults instead of arguing children had told him a lot. Roman turned up the heat to make sure Melody didn't get cold. "I'm glad you think so. I was worried about taking you away from your friends."

"It's not as though we can't go back to visit. In fact, I've already convinced Emersyn that she and Gabe will need to take a vacation out here next summer." Melody leaned against him, grinning as she kept her eyes glued to the windows.

Moving out of Sheridan proper, Austin turned down a side road and headed out into the country. Roman felt himself relaxing more and more as they drove, finding comfort and familiarity in a bump or pothole here and a tree there. He'd known he belonged there the first time he'd arrived, but at that time in his life, he'd never imagined he'd be bringing his one true mate back home with him. He kept his arms wrapped around her, determined never to let her go again.

"Here we are," Austin announced as he pulled into the driveway.

"No way." Melody scrambled out of the truck before Roman could insist on helping her down. "You didn't tell me you lived in a log cabin!"

Roman had simply seen it as a house before, but everything about him had changed, including his perspective. He could see why Melody would have loved the place, with the split-rail fence around the front yard, the stone foundation, and the heavy logs that made up the home. He'd been more focused on the huge pole barn off to the side that allowed him a place to work from and keep his equipment, but Melody herself was all about home. Now that she was there, he couldn't imagine the place without her.

"It's not locked. You can head on in, and I'll be there in a second." Roman could barely finish his sentence before she'd trotted up the porch steps.

"You've got yourself an enthusiastic one there," Austin noted as he helped pull the luggage out of the truck's bed. "She seems sweet, too, not like some of the girls I've met recently."

"You must like her, considering how civil you're being," Roman noted. "I know you're not a fan of having strangers around." He'd witnessed Austin react when some tourists had accidentally come up Austin's driveway, then were promptly escorted out by the wrong end of a shotgun.

"If she's your mate, then she's part of the clan. That's different, not like these city slickers my sister wants to bring in after converting the whole damn place to a dude ranch like the Bancrofts did." He turned his head and spat on the ground.

Roman shrugged and smiled. "I had to go halfway across the country to find her, if that tells you anything."

"The bigger miracle is that you convinced her to come up here to the middle of nowhere and live with a lout like you," Austin said with a grin.

"You just go on home and be jealous, then. I've got to get settled in and give Melody the grand tour." Roman made a shooing motion down the driveway.

Austin waggled his brows suggestively. "I see how it is. I should be getting home, though. The dogs will be upset that I've left the house without them for a change." With the last of the bags out of the truck, Austin hopped back into the driver's seat and fired up the engine.

Roman leaned in the window. Everyone down at Force HQ in L.A. knew about the good news, but it was going to spread fast enough around Sheridan. "I've been so busy traveling that I didn't get a chance to tell you we're expecting a little one next summer."

"You lucky son of a bitch!" Austin clapped him on the arm and grasped his hand. "Congratulations! Man, I hope I'm lucky enough to find my mate at some point. Some of these cold nights get pretty lonely, but I guess you wouldn't know about that."

"Not anymore. I can't wait to introduce her to the rest of the clan. I think she's going to fit in well." Roman glanced toward the house, eager to get back to her.

"She will. I'll put together a New Year's Eve party up at my house, and I'll be sure to stock something non-alcoholic for her." Austin put the truck in reverse and waved as he backed out of the driveway.

Roman headed inside to find Melody standing in the middle of the living room. She looked so happy as she turned to him, her hair bouncing as she jogged across the rug to put her arms around him. "Roman, this place is great! I know it's past Christmas, but I can already see just how beautiful we can make it next December. I love the open floor plan and all the wood, and there's plenty of room for the baby."

He nodded as he pulled her into his arms. Roman couldn't remember ever having such a sense of home and family, and they'd only been there for a few minutes. "There's a room right next to the master bedroom that's perfect for a nursery."

"Perfect, just like you." Melody kissed him, and then she kissed him again.

He pulled her closer, deepening the kiss. The house was cool from being unoccupied for the last month, but he felt his own body heating up. He'd been looking forward to having some alone time with her. "I can't wait to show you the place. This house is on clan land, and all the ranching area that expands between the houses is shared by all of us. I also can't wait for them to meet you, but first, I'd like to give you a very detailed tour of that master bedroom. I plan on the two of us spending a lot of time in there, at least as much as we can before the baby comes."

She bit her lower lip as she looked up at him, but she backed away and let go. "We can do that soon enough, but there's something I've got to do first."

"What's that?"

Melody bent over toward one of the suitcases he'd just brought in and unzipped it. "I think your house is absolutely lovely, but I'd like to start giving it my own touch when it comes to décor."

Roman blinked. "All right."

She stood, holding a small jar in her hands. Melody confidently crossed the room and put it on the mantel.

Stepping closer, Roman saw that it was full of the rose petals he'd given her when he'd come back to L.A. "That's nice, but I think it needs something more."

"Really?" It was Melody's turn to be surprised.

"Definitely." He unzipped his own bag and removed the tiny stocking. "It might be past Christmas for this year, but I don't mind having a little something put up." He hung it on a hook just beneath the jar full of petals. "What do you think?"

She slipped her arms around him once again, a gesture that was natural to them already. "I love it, and I love you. I think it's time to check out that master bedroom you mentioned."

Roman took her hands and led the way, eager to start their new life together.

THE END

If you enjoyed *Santa Soldier Bear*, get ready for Austin's story, the first book in the new Wild Frontier Shifters series! Read on for a sneak peek of *Her Rancher Bear*.

AUSTIN

"Ow! Dammit, Roman! You get my fingers with that hammer again, and you'll be pushing up daisies out in the pasture," Austin warned, holding the barbed wire in place.

"I said I was sorry," Roman grumbled. "Maybe if your big ol' paws weren't in the way—"

"You know what they say about big hands."

Roman shook his head. "Whatever you say, man. Can we wrap this up already? I've gotta go check on Melody. She's about to have that baby any day now."

Austin tucked the fencing pliers into the back pocket of his jeans and stood back, looking at their work as Izzy and Dizzy chased each other around a fencepost. His mother's two Boston Terriers loved coming along for the ranch work, whether Austin wanted them there or not. They did have their purpose, but more often than not, they were underfoot. "I suppose that'll do for now."

"For now?" Roman rested his hand on the nearest fencepost, surveying the row of freshly-repaired posts along the cattle pasture. The grass had turned green and lush under the Wyoming summer sun. "I know I haven't been in this business for generations like you have, but it looks pretty damn good to me."

"It does," Austin agreed. Roman was right. He'd come into ranching and into their clan about a year ago when he'd left the military. He'd proven himself to be a hard worker and a family man, one who'd seen the temptations of city life, yet still returned to the place he now called home in Sheridan, Wyoming. Austin had to give him credit for that, and for always being willing to help. He did like to rib him for not being a rancher, born-and-raised, but Roman gave him hell right back when he accused Austin of never seeing a single blade of grass outside of his own territory.

"There's nothing wrong with the fence at all," Austin continued. "I'm sure it would stand the test of time if left to its own devices. But I'm not convinced that the Bancroft clan wasn't behind this. Ever since they opened that damn dude ranch, they've been trying to sabotage everything we have going on here." He wanted to spit every time he thought about it.

Roman rubbed his lips together. "Sounds like a big problem."

"It is."

"Have you talked to Levi?" The Alpha of their clan also happened to be the local sheriff.

Austin pulled in a deep breath. "A little. He knows what's been happening, but I don't have any actual proof. I told him I could handle it. He's probably got enough on his hands dealing with that brother of his."

Roman chuckled. "Wade got himself in trouble again?"

"That's what I understand. I never should've listened when Shawna suggested we turn this place into a dude ranch. She insisted the numbers were on her side, and I didn't see any way out of it." He pulled in a deep breath as he wondered what his ancestors might think of the commercialized, touristy operation they were now running. At least it was a lot more rustic than some of the other ranches that catered solely to city slickers. The Crawford Ranch was still a family-centered place that focused on raising cattle and doing things the old-fashioned way, just how he liked it. He didn't like having nosy humans roaming around his territory, and he absolutely hated it when they wanted to follow him around and see how the work was done, but the money it brought in was hard to argue with.

Checking his watch, Roman gestured to his truck parked nearby. "I'd better get going. I don't want to be away from Melody any longer than I need to be right now."

"Sure thing. Keep me updated. And thanks for the help." Austin turned to Gunner, his chestnut gelding who patiently waited nearby. He swung easily up into the saddle and headed back down to the barn, Izzy and Dizzy keeping up in the dust clouds behind him. It'd been a long, hot day. Austin was already behind on his daily chores, and as he got closer to the center of operations, he remembered he was supposed to have guests coming that afternoon.

He cursed under his breath. He didn't have time for this. He spent far too many hours showing tourists around and coming up with activities to keep them entertained, as if they weren't grown-ass adults who could take care of themselves.

On top of the many other jobs he had at the

ranch, making sure the guests didn't get bored was the worst. He removed Gunner's tack and gave him a good rubdown while the two dogs competed over a hoof clipping from the last time the farrier had been there. Austin shooed them toward the house before he headed for the outdoor shower stall at the back of the barn. He was covered in horse dirt and cattle mud, and if he didn't track it into the house, he'd have one less thing to take care of.

Austin stripped off his clothes and tossed them aside on a nearby bench, but he carefully hung his Stetson on a hook on the outside wall of the shower. He stood directly under the showerhead as he turned on the spigot, not bothering to wait for it to heat up. There was something about that first spray of bitterly cold water that woke him up and reminded him of just where and who he was. He was a rancher. He was a survivor. He was out there in the middle of nowhere, with no one around, and that was just the way he liked it.

Grabbing a bar of soap, he began washing away the dirt, along with his worries about opening the family ranch to strangers, letting his concerns go running down the drain in the center of the concrete shower floor. Sure, these folks could bankrupt him if they did something stupid, but they could also make his family a good living if they brought all their friends. In the moment, he was happy to not think about any of it.

He stiffened as he felt someone watching him. No, it was something deeper than that. Something affected him all the way down to his core, making his inner grizzly raise its head and pay attention.

A long whistle sounded behind him. "I knew we were coming out here to see how they raise cattle, but they obviously do a hell of a job with their cowboys, too."

Austin rinsed the soap out of his eyes and glanced over his shoulder to find three ladies standing there, staring at him in shock. "Shit!" He grabbed a towel from a nearby hook and wrapped it around his waist. These must have been the guests that were supposed to be staying for the week. "I didn't expect you for another few hours."

The woman in the middle's cheeks were flushed, her lips slightly parted, but the gaze from her deep green eyes was unwavering. She didn't bother to check out his rugged physique as the other women were doing, choosing to stare deep into his soul instead. Not a strand of her deep golden hair was out of place, and her fitted dress suggested she thought she'd be spending the afternoon at a luxury hotel instead of a farmstead. She blinked as though she were coming out of a trance and then looked away.

"I...I'm sorry. Our earlier plans fell through, so we went ahead and came right here. We didn't find anyone up by the house, so..." Her voice was deep and velvety, and it sent a quiver of energy through Austin's stomach.

He returned her level stare, only vaguely aware of the other women standing there. He wasn't particularly modest, having grown up in a rural area where getting things done was the important thing, and there was no room for shyness. Regardless, he knew he'd feel naked under her gaze, even if he were fully clothed.

"Don't be sorry, Harper," purred the woman to her left, the one who'd initially spoken. She openly eyed Austin's broad chest without a hint of impropriety showing in her eyes. "If you ask me, this is going to get the Crawford Ranch a five-star review."

"Oh my god, can we just go?" asked the third woman, shielding her eyes and edging away from the scene. "This is so embarrassing!"

Either Harper simply wasn't impressed, or she was too cool to let him know. She kept her gaze carefully averted as she edged away. "We'll go now. We're looking for someone named Austin."

"Well, you've found him." Tucking in the corner of his towel, Austin sighed and grabbed his hat, gesturing around the corner of the barn toward the house. "You can head into the lodge and I'll be there in a moment." He couldn't help himself as he stared at the blonde. His inner grizzly was stirring, impatient, eager to get closer to her. He stepped out of the shower, meaning to head toward the back of the house, but he brushed past her on his way.

Austin could hear the other women giggling and arguing as they went around to the front, but he could still feel Harper's eyes on him.

No doubt, this was going to be a long week.

ALSO BY MEG RIPLEY
ALL AVAILABLE ON AMAZON

Shifter Nation Universe

Wild Frontier Shifters

Book 1: Her Rancher Bear

Special Ops Shifters: L.A. Force Series

Book 1: Secret Baby For The Soldier Bear

Book 2: Saved By The Soldier Dragon

Book 3: Bonded To The Soldier Wolf

Book 4: Forbidden Mate For The Soldier Bear

Book 5: Bride For The Soldier Bear

Book 6: Feral Soldier Wolf

Book 7: Santa Soldier Bear

Special Ops Shifters: Dallas Force Series

Book 1: Rescued By The Soldier Bear

Book 2: Protected By The Soldier Tiger

Book 3: Fated To The Soldier Fox

Book 4: Baby For The Soldier Cougar

Special Ops Shifters Series (original D.C. Force)

Book 1: Daddy Soldier Bear

Book 2: Fake Mate For The Soldier Lion

Book 3: Captured By The Soldier Wolf

Book 4: Christmas With The Soldier Dragon

Werebears of Acadia Series

Werebears of the Everglades Series

Werebears of Glacier Bay Series

Werebears of Big Bend Series

Dragons of Charok Universe

Daddy Dragon Guardians Series

Shifters Between Worlds Series

More Shifter Romances

Forever Fated Mates Box Set

Shifter Daddies Box Set

Beverly Hills Dragons Series

Dragons of Sin City Series

Dragons of the Darkblood Secret Society Series

Packs of the Pacific Northwest Series

<u>Early Short Stories</u>

Mated By The Dragon Boss

Claimed By The Werebears of Green Tree

Bearer of Secrets

Rogue Wolf

ABOUT THE AUTHOR

Meg Ripley is an author of steamy shifter romances. A Seattle native, Meg can often be found curled up in a local coffee house with her laptop.

Download Meg's entire *Caught Between Dragons* series when you sign up for her newsletter!

Sign up by visiting www.redlilypublishing.com or Meg's Facebook page:
https://www.facebook.com/authormegripley/

Printed in Great Britain
by Amazon